Crunchy Life
Hoop Dreams

Written by

Glen Mourning

GLEN MOURNING

DEDICATION

In a world full of challenges, children may have it the hardest when it comes to learning how to make the most out of life. And when you are fortunate enough to make it to adulthood, remember that along the way, some grown-ups cared deeply for you. This book is dedicated to kids and hard-working adults who want to make the world a better place.

ACKNOWLEDGMENTS

To my mother, Lillian
Without your support and unconditional love, I would have indeed given up on myself as a young man and as a student. Attending school was challenging, but when I learned how education could open the door to a better tomorrow, I learned to wake up each morning with a purpose. You made me believe in me! Thank you to all of the fantastic parents, guardians, teachers, coaches, and mentors around the world. Your efforts are necessary and appreciated.

Never give up.
Success is on the other side of your struggle.

Reading Standard question stems for developing strong independent thinkers

Why did (event) happen? How do you know? • What does (character) think about (event)? How do you know? • What do you think (character) will do differently next time? • Explain why (character or object) is important to the story.

What happened at the beginning, middle, and end of the story? • What is a summary of this story? • What is the lesson you should learn from this story? • What is this story trying to teach?

How does (character) feel at this part of the story? How do you know? • How does (character) actions change what happens in the story? • What problem does (character) have in the story? How does he/she solve their problem? • How does (character) change throughout the story? • What are (character) personality traits? How does his/ her personality affect what happens in the story? • Why is the setting important to the story?

How are the parts of the story connected? How does this section/chapter help the reader understand the setting? • How does this scene build suspense? • How would you retell this story, including important parts from the beginning, middle, and end? • In poetry, what stanza is the most interesting to you? Why? • Why did the author organize the story like this? How would it be different if the order were changed?

Who is telling this story? How do you know? • Are the narrator and the author the same person? How do you know? • From what point of view is this written? • What does (character/narrator) think of (event/action)? What do you think? What would you have done differently?

Sometimes... life gets a little crunchy!

Introduction

Elite Public Charter School or EPCS, as it will often be referred to as, is a fictional charter school located in Washington, D.C. The characters and their families are based on real-life people and events.

Sometimes, life isn't as smooth or as safe as we would want it to be. Sometimes, life can get a little challenging, a little discouraging, and a little *crunchy*. Just keep on living and doing what you can to find success through all of the struggles. Just keep on chewing away. It'll always get better if you believe it will. Never give up hope.

As a ten-year old girl growing up in Southeast, Washington, D.C, Alyah Marie had seen a lot of crazy things. But then again, no one ever said that life would be easy for kids growing up in big cities. First, there were the big State Test that most kids feared and never experienced any success from taking them. Then, there was the violence that took place on a daily basis in the neighborhoods. The noise of police sirens, fire trucks and ambulance vehicles drowned out any sounds of hope for her community.

To add on to that, there were the bullies that kids had to face every day. And like it or not, standing your ground was something you had to do to avoid being the laughingstock of your class.

If that doesn't sound like enough stress for a kid, there was also the thought that at any moment your teacher might decide that they've had enough frustration from teaching a disruptive group of kids and quit, leaving a class of kids behind without even saying goodbye.

Until this school year, Alyah had been given every reason to believe that life for her and her mother Viola was *normal*. She started her elementary school career thinking that all the other kids lived at home with certain fears and worries of growing up in the *hood*.

Even though she was ten-years old, she had assumed that everyone lived like her. She believed that all kids lived with their moms and that all of the dads in the world were separated and *distant* from their families.

In her neighborhood it was common to see women running the households without any help from a man. Growing up Alyah watched women carry the groceries into their apartments without any help. She saw moms change flat tires by themselves. And for five days a week she watched women and even older sisters carefully walk their younger family members to school.

Alyah would come to believe that maybe the men in her neighborhood were just picked on more or left behind without any help from the people that they needed. Somehow the men in her neighborhood managed to always get involved with the wrong crowds of people. And because of that, it was normal for Alyah to see police cars with black men sitting in the back seats.

Alyah was growing up to think that most black men usually landed in jail or were at least somehow kicked out of their homes for reasons that she didn't understand.

The next phase of her young life was about to begin. She was now old enough and smart enough to tell when something wasn't right. She developed a desire to want to help others. This year she would be entering the fifth grade and would be challenged like never before. Her experiences allowed her to conclude that it was somehow *okay* for the boys in her class to act out and get themselves into trouble. She then began to believe that it was *normal* to be bothered and yelled at by all the boys at school.

Alyah's environment had made it hard for her to believe that a kid like her could actually change what was happening in her neighborhood. But her mother was unlike anyone that she had ever known. Viola Ramsey was extremely encouraging and motivating to her daughter.

As the fifth grade got underway, Alyah began to believe that it was possible to bring positivity to her community.

That was until the bad news made its way to room 227. One of the fifth-grade teachers at EPCS was having the most difficult time of her teaching career. Only three weeks had passed since the first day of school and the behaviors were getting worse every day.

The kids screamed and threw paper balls around the room. They got out of their seats without permission and most of the boys said the meanest things to almost everyone in class. Worst of all, no one seemed to be doing any classwork or learning, besides Alyah. She had been the only student handing in assignments and completing activities for her teacher. However, before the 3rd week of September came to an end, Ms. Brown quit teaching.

It could not have happened at a more crucial point in Alyah and Viola's lives. Over the past summer Viola realized that she wasn't going to be able to afford to send Alyah back to Sidwell.

Alyah had just transferred back to Elite Public Charter School where she dreaded returning to after realizing that a private school education was out of the picture.

She didn't remember much about kindergarten and first grade, but second grade memories often replayed in her mind. For the past two years as a third and fourth grader she had been a student at one of the best schools in the country and now she was back to her neighborhood school where it all began for her. Alyah was bright and had incredible potential but private school tuition was no longer something her mother could afford.

Ms. Brown's decision left Alyah heartbroken as Alyah had immediately gravitated towards Ms. Brown's young and ambitious heart and soul. The decision to quit left the fifth graders in room 227 stranded without the one person who Alyah assumed would have been able to help her reimagine a brighter future.

It wasn't the first time that a teacher had left her or decided that teaching her class was too hard for them to do.

One day, when Alyah was in the second grade, her teacher Ms. Kettles screamed so loud that Alyah thought her teacher's head was going to explode. She had been bitten on her arm by one of the boys in the class and had decided that the incident was the final straw. If being bitten on the arm doesn't seem like a big deal, every single day that she had come to work, Ms. Kettles was hit or screamed at by one of Alyah's classmates. That was what her classes had been like from kindergarten until second grade which made dysfunction and chaos seem normal to Alyah.

Shortly after Ms. Kettles quit teaching, Alyah's class experienced different substitute teachers every week. Sometimes the class misbehaved to the point of even causing the substitute teachers to pack up their bags and run out of the building without ever looking back.

With the struggles of being provided a quality education, Alyah's mom was desperate. She had never really gotten any help from Alyah's father but at that point in time, she had no choice but to reach out for support.

Alyah's mother didn't know much about teaching but being a practicing lawyer in D.C helped her realized that those conditions were not going to help any child learn and that her own daughter deserved so much better.

The problem was that it would cost entirely too much for Viola to send her daughter to a school where the students were well behaved, where the teachers didn't fear for their safety and where teachers loved going in to work. Families like Viola and Alyah would need a ton of help in order to attend such a school.

It was clear that Alyah's mom wanted the best for her and that she wanted nothing more than for Alyah to go to the best school in D.C. But she was raising Alyah all alone. In any case, Viola wasn't making enough money to send her daughter to an expensive private school for the long haul.

As time moved on and Alyah finished the second grade, Viola called on Alyah's father for help. Alyah's father Tyler Weston, had left Viola when Alyah was born and moved to live outside of New York City. Although it had been years since they had last spoken or seen each other, Viola saw no other solution in order to do what was right for their daughter.

The issue wasn't simply that Viola would be asking Tyler for money to help pay for their daughter's education. The worst part of the situation would be convincing Tyler that Viola wasn't the person that his family told him she was back in the day.

Tyler's family had convinced him that Viola, who was a Black woman, only loved him, a White man, because he was going to be rich and famous. Although he never truly believed it, he still had a fear that people only liked him because of his money and fame.

Tyler's dad had fed him lies for years to help break the two of them apart. Tyler continued struggling to believe that Viola's love for him was real. When she finally decided to reach out for help, she didn't want to remind Tyler of the people who had hurt him and broke his heart. He never got over the pain from having only been appreciated by his own family *after* making it big.

Back In The Day

Tyler Weston was a former NBA basketball player who was born and raised in Maryland. After attending Georgetown University, he went on to play for three NBA teams before finally settling down to live a normal and peaceful life. During his time in the spotlight, his family members had begged him for money and made him feel like money was the only reason people showed their love for him. And because of that, he shut people out of his life.

Before attending Georgetown, his father had been known for making rude and disrespectful comments about other races of people, especially towards Black Americans. Tyler had known since he was a kid that his dad felt a particular way about the boys he hung out with and the ones that he played basketball with at the parks. He would often warn Tyler to stick with his own kind and never allowed any of Tyler's Black teammates to come over the house to hang out.

As a result of those experiences, Tyler grew up despising his father, but appreciating his Black brothers more than any other group. He had only known his friends to be kind, caring loving and most of all, accepting of him as a member of their crew. Tyler then grew up with respect for all people and carried those values with him as he had headed off to pursue his basketball career.

Tyler went off to attend Georgetown University as he was one of only two white basketball players on the entire team during his years of playing hoops. He and Viola had first met during their college journeys when Viola was finishing Law School at Howard University. During her senior year, Viola was in charge of a social justice peace group on campus that was known throughout the region for uniting people from other colleges.

At one of her peace marches at Georgetown, she had met a tall and handsome, blue eyed basketball star who wanted nothing more than to help spread peace and positivity around the world. After Tyler met Viola, he learned about what she was doing for people. After that, he began to run his own marches and meetings on Georgetown's campus to promote social justice.

The two of them had joined teams and met up a few more times to encourage change in the D.C area. The two activists soon fell in love as Tyler and Viola would continue promoting equality and education for students and people of color.

Tyler and Viola continued working side by side as social justice advocates and brought up issues for people to fix such as access to health care, police brutality against minorities and homelessness.

Although they both contributed to society, they were in the fight for justice for two different reasons. Tyler joined the fight for equal rights because he had always known that life for some people in America wasn't fair. Viola on the other hand, fought for those who she loved such as the people in her own family and for those in the neighborhood that she herself lived in.

Although he was a White American, he knew deep down inside that there was something he could do to help make life better for his black and brown brothers and sisters.

Luck had brought them together and it was love at first sight. As soon as they realized that Alyah was going to be born they then planned on being together forever. Life between them was great.

But Tyler had family members who didn't agree with his stance on racial issues. His family never understood why he tried helping people who didn't look like him. His family became upset that he spent so much time in the Black community and so little time with them.

And just before he planned on asking Viola to marry him, his mother and father explained that they would stop loving him based on his choice of wanting to spend his life married to and raising a family with an African American woman.

Tyler's family was *different* from Viola's family. Although Viola's family knew that she was in love with a white man, they still showed Tyler love and respect because of how great he treated Viola. Although Tyler loved all people regardless of the color of their skin, his family had a harder time accepting *others*.

Tyler never understood why his parents acted the way that they did. All he knew for sure was that his mother and father were both from the south and that they never seemed to care to get along with other races of people.

Instead, they made sure that he removed himself from Viola's life without reasonable explanations. Then when Tyler refused to listen to them right way, his parents went as far as making up a story that messed with Tyler's mind for years. They created the illusion in Tyler's mind about how Viola only wanted to marry him for his money and fame. Tyler never truly believed it, but the drama left Viola devastated as her and Tyler were forced to go their separate ways.

When Tyler reported to play in his first season in the NBA, he continued advocating for equal rights as a spokesperson and professional athlete. He and his teammates lead marches to unite people of all races during his time in the spotlight.

Sadly, his daughter Alyah would be left to grow up without her father. The truth about what happened when she was a baby was never shared with her. Her mom never talked about who her father was or why he and her never stayed together.

Although Tyler only played professional basketball for five seasons, he was fortunate enough to save a few million dollars for having played in the NBA. However, this made him a target for family members to beg him for money and cars and for his help. Because of his fear of being taken advantage of, he moved away from Maryland and the D.C area which is where his family lived. At the age of thirty-two, he decided that a quiet life in a suburban neighborhood outside of New York City would be the perfect place to escape from his annoying relatives.

Knowing how much Tyler hated being bothered by his family members, Viola chose to never bother Tyler about money because she didn't want him to think that money was all she wanted.

She wanted to prove to him that she was in fact different than his own family.

Therefore, she raised Alyah on her own and to the best of her ability. From time to time, Tyler would remind Viola that when the time came, he would be sure to support Alyah through college in order to help her when she becomes a young woman. But waiting until Alyah got older seemed like he didn't care about the present time.

As for now and during her elementary school days, both Tyler and Viola kept their distance and barely ever spoke to one another about Alyah or about anything.

Moving On

Fortunately for Alyah, her father wasn't the only successful parent. Viola was a successful woman. As a lawyer, there were several big-time court cases that she had taken on and won. Her big wins as a lawyer came with earning a ton of money that she saved to raise her daughter.

One case that she worked on was for a Black teenaged boy named Nasir Brown. Everyone knew Nasir as Nas, the next NBA superstar in the making. He was from Viola's neighborhood and had been known to be a great young man. What happened to Nas was a tragedy. The bright, and talented young man was murdered by a police officer which created a nationwide uprising against the mistreatment of people of color in America by law enforcement.

Viola had known for her entire life that things like what happened to Nas were an unfortunate symptom of racism in America. During an afternoon one summer, Nasir was walking home from basketball practice and had been mistaken for another Black teen. Nasir had *somewhat* resembled a young man who had been involved in several crimes in the D.C area.

Although the two young men may have looked alike, what took place was beyond devastating. A mother lost a son, a community lost a great young man and a beautiful Black boy lost his life, all because of a mistaken identify.

On the day of his death, Nasir left basketball practice to walk home as he did every day. On his way home, a short and slightly overweight white man saw him and pulled his car over to talk to him. As the man got out of the car, witnesses said that Nas seemed afraid and unsure what to do. The man then got out of his car and walked over to Nasir who was still dribbling his basketball.

Few words seemed to have been exchanged according to a young woman who was standing on the other side of the street when the off-duty cop approached him. Unsure of how to respond, Nasir allegedly asked the man to back up and get out of his face. Nas had no idea why the man was following him and asked the man what it was that he wanted from him.

Nas played on multiple basketball teams and most people recognized him right away as an up and coming star athlete in the D.C area. He had been playing on an all-star team that held practices in a private school gymnasium that happened to be in a gentrified area of Southwest D.C. The *former* cop later mentioned to TV reporters that it was uncommon to see black teenagers walk around the neighborhood in hooded sweatshirts, even if the hoody bore the logo of the team that Nas played for.

At the time of their altercation, all that the cop had saw was a black teen who fit a *description* and who he thought shouldn't be anywhere near an affluent neighborhood at that time of day. The two men supposedly got into an argument over Nas not answering any of the man's questions and then trying to walk away. The witness said that the man then reached for Nas' hoody, perhaps so that the man could get a better look at him.

As Nas refused to obey the cop's command, he shifted his gym bag in what could have been an attempt to take out his student player I.D badge to show the man. At that moment, the cop panicked, and the situation ended with Nasir dead on the street from one fatal gun shot wound.

The case carried on for several months. Viola demanded justice for Nas and his family and for changes to be made. She wanted to ensure that cops would be better prepared to address unarmed people, especially innocent Black teenagers. Nas and the cop were not filmed by anyone holding a smart phone which may have made it easier for her to win the case.

However, as a lawyer and as a mother of a Black child, Viola had seen several cases where the crime had been caught on camera and a white man walked free. She began to believe that because of the color of a victim's skin, even with that type of evidence pointing to a corrupt individual, somehow cases still ended without bringing justice to the communities. She was tired of losing young people from her community to irresponsible cops that used unnecessary brutality.

Viola had every right to fear that Nasir's case may have not received any justice. Television shows were full of clips of the off-duty cop trying to explain to the media why he shot and killed an unarmed teenager. The TV shows also only highlighted negative information about Nasir.

During the trial the media failed to mention that Nas was on track to become the next NBA superstar as well as the fact that he was a mentor to other kids in the neighborhood who were growing up without their fathers. One reporter even mentioned that back when Nas was ten-years old, he got in trouble for fighting in school, as if to show that he was a bad kid.

For months people tried understanding how something like Nasir's death could have even happened.

The city was furious for a long time and people were heartbroken over the fact that Nasir was simply walking home from the gym. Nasir's family sued the city and thankfully received justice for their son in the process.

Viola worked several other high-profile court cases and won justice for several clients. Due to how great of a lawyer she was, she was able to make enough money to have the option to send her daughter to a top school.

For the third and forth-grade school years, Viola made the call to pay for Alyah to go to private school. Although she had saved enough to pay for her fees and the cost of tuition, it eventually got so expensive that it came down to either moving to a cheaper and more dangerous part of the city or putting her back in her old school. By sending Alyah back to public school, the two of them would have at least been able to afford living somewhere that wasn't extremely rough and violent.

In the 2nd grade, Alyah was reading well ahead of not only her classmates at Elite Public Charter School, but her test scores also put her ahead of most kids in entire country. It was hard to say whether or not Alyah was a genius or anything, but she definitely loved reading.

And so, for two years she was able to attend Sidwell and Friends School. Now if you don't know how significant that is, just consider these facts. It's the school where the President of The

United States and really rich and famous people send their kids.

Unfortunately for Alyah and Viola, a school like Sidwell was not something that they could afford all on their own. Luckily, for the first year while Alyah was in third-grade, Viola was able to rely on her savings that she earned while working on some of her biggest cases as a lawyer.

Although Alyah successfully completed the third-grade, it didn't take long for Viola's savings to run out, requiring her to look for additional financial support.

Viola had combined all the money that she had saved from before Alyah was born with the earnings from her large court cases. As the money finally ran out, so did Alyah's time as a third grader at Sidwell.

Viola's back was against the wall. She would have to finally put her pride aside and ask Tyler for help. Fortunately, he immediately realized how important it was going to be for Alyah to attend the best school in the city. It was clear to Tyler that Viola had sacrificed everything in order to prepare Alyah for success.

Tyler made the choice to help Viola out but was unable to guarantee that Alyah would be able to remain in a private school. With the help of her father, Alyah was able to attend Sidwell as a fourth grader.

Girl With The Dream

Told by Alyah

Before I switched schools and started going
to Sidwell my mom used to baby sit my cousin
Dajuan. My mom and his mom Shantell were only
one year apart. Everyone from around the way
thought that they were sisters. My mom used to tell
me stories about how they would tell everyone in
the neighborhood that they were twins.

Shantell and my mom became parents
around the same time. That's why me and my
cousin Dajuan have always been close. Me and
Dajuan had gone to school with each other since

kindergarten. Most people thought that we were twins, too. He and his mom lived right across the street with his grandmother. Each and every day my mom would honk the horn at the exact same time, letting Shantell know to bring him downstairs so that my mom could bring us both to school.

Dajuan and I were never in the same classroom at EPCS but we ate lunch together, played at recess together and always took a family picture during sibling picture day. Shantell and my mom were always nice to each other and my mom did everything she could to help Shantell raise Dajuan.

Like my dad, Dajuan's dad was away. He wasn't just in another state, living life far away like my dad was doing. Dajuan's dad was in prison. I don't know if Dajuan ever goes to see his dad, but I don't think it's my business to worry about that. As soon as my mom made the choice to send me to Sidwell, her and Shantell stopped speaking to each other. I wasn't sure but it had seemed like they were in a big fight.

One day, Shantell really needed a babysitter but my mom had to change her schedule in order to make everything work for us. We had to leave earlier to drive me to school and she picked me up later because of the afterschool activities. This left Shantell without the help that she was used to having. Then, one morning while my mom watched me put my seatbelt on in the back seat of the car, I saw Shantell racing down the stairs to come over to the car.

"Hey, cuz...I need you today. We...need you today", cried Shantell.

"Shantell, I know how hard it might be for you to get used to this, but you are gonna have to figure out what to do," cried my mom.

Both my mom and Shantell stood there in silence, without saying anything to each other for a moment. And then...Shantell exploded.

"You think your daughter is better than my son or something?" asked Shantell. "If I could afford to send him to some fancy, white people school, I'd send him, too. But just because you send your baby to a good school don't mean that y'all are better than us", shouted Shantell.

As Shantell voiced her frustration my mom double checked to make sure that the car doors were shut. I guess she didn't want me to hear their conversation, but it was hard not to.

Without spending much time arguing, my mom simply told Shantell that she'd see her later and that she loved her. Just then, we sped off and made our way to Sidwell.

There were a bunch of other moments like that where my mom experienced people making her feel bad for wanting the best for me. She didn't let it bother her, or at least she didn't let me see if any of it bothered her.

There I was, able to take classes in the 3rd and 4th grade that prepared me for middle school and even high school. I received basketball lessons during after school activities and was preparing to ask my mom if I could play for the Sidwell middle school team once I was old enough.

Just from P.E class alone, I became known as the best athlete in the entire school. Kids at school also started to notice how great of a reader I was.

Somehow, students also found out that my mom was a lawyer. During lunch, kids often asked me how rich my mom was and assumed that my family was wealthy and famous like the Obama's or like Lebron James' family or something. But the truth was that my mom was born on Alabama Avenue in D.C and that she was the oldest child of her two late parents, Mr. and Mrs. Elijah Ramsey. No one knew that my mom grew up in the projects. But she didn't let her circumstances stop her from becoming a highly educated queen, okay!

I never managed to explain much to kids at Sidwell about my mom or about other people in my family. One day for an assignment in fourth grade we had to write about our family history. The assignment required me to ask my grandparents questions in order to write a story.

Finishing that task was tricky for me. I never had a chance to meet my grandparents because they both passed away when my mother was in college. My grandmother died of cancer when my mom started college at Howard University and my grandfather, well…he was taken from my mom in a way more tragic than being sick.

After my grandmother died my mom said that my grandfather dedicated the rest of his life to working. For years he did double shifts, I guess to keep his mind off of having lost the love of his life. But then, something crazy happened to him. One night, after a long day of work, my grandfather was gunned down in a senseless act of violence on his way home. He worked as a security guard at Walter Reed Medical center and dedicated his life to making sure that my mom would have the best chances at life. Ever since I was a baby my mom had told me why she wanted to become a lawyer. She told me how when they found the person who took my grandfather's life that they let him go because the man who was the lawyer during the trial didn't do his job to ensure that justice would be served. The lawyer didn't get all the necessary evidence. Instead, the lawyer was unprepared and couldn't support the argument and eventually lost the case. My mom made it seem like the lawyer, who was a white man, didn't even care about the case and had seemed to only be there because it was his job instead of actually caring to help put the bad man away.

But back to how things turned out for me. After my first year at Sidwell, my mother met a woman who recognized how dedicated she was at helping me become the best child that I could be. The lady happened to be the assistant to a big-time brain surgeon in D.C and the two of them became great friends.

My mom's friend knew people in high places which meant that she was able to help my mom out when it came to tuition. My mom, however, wasn't someone who wanted people to feel sorry for her or for us or to be given handouts. My grandfather taught my mom to be honest and to earn her keep. But when my mom realized how scared I was to be in a classroom where kids were misbehaving every second and where teachers were quitting left and right, she knew that she had no choice but to allow someone to help her. My mom put her pride aside for as long as she could. And so for two full years, with the help from my mom's new friend along with the money from my dad, I attended the best school in the country.

On days when my mom couldn't pick me up on time, her friend Mrs. Durkin volunteered to help my mom out. Once or twice during the week, Mrs. Durkin would bring me home or allow me to attend her daughter's tennis practice. Sometimes, my mom picked me up from the private tennis lessons that Mrs. Durkin's daughter Pamela received.

I was thankful for the help that I got during those days, but nothing was as great as the rides to school that my mom and I took. Before each of those 60-minute rides to school from Southeast to Maryland, my mom prayed over me before we headed out to the car. "Dear Heavenly Father, be our shield and guide me. Protect my daughter from harm and from the evils of the world. I pray that you give us protection and love us. We thank you for all that you do. Amen".

My mom would then shuffle me out the front door. Once in the car and on the road, I paid attention to the whole world around me. Less than 50 feet from our front door was a liquor store where older Black men, in shaggy clothes walked back and forth and sat on milk crates, entertaining each other with conversation and handshakes.

If we got stuck at the light before making the turn onto Martin Luther King Jr. Avenue, I would role my window down to try to hear what they laughed and joked about.

I was never successful at that at all.

As we drove down the street, homeless men and women lined the fence along an abandoned fish market. I didn't know who they were or why they lived outside…on the ground, but my mom always told me to never make fun of them but to pray for their peace and safety instead. There were three schools in the area, which is why before we got onto the highway, I'd see students in their school uniforms walking to their schools. As the kids from my neighborhood walked to school with their siblings and their moms, for those two years that we passed them on the way to school, I wondered if they loved their school as much as I loved being a student at Sidwell.

I wondered if they saw the abandoned homes, torn and tattered property that once belonged to powerful and brilliant Black families in the same way that I saw them? To me, the poor and destroyed areas meant that someone was needed to fix them, to bring them back to life, to somehow make them *better.*

I wondered if when police cars and ambulance trucks sped by us early in the morning, if the kids who also saw the emergency response teams thought to themselves that one day they could become doctors and surgeons and make sure that the people in our community are taken care of? I wondered if…the kids who made their way to school…like my cousin Dajuan…even ever wondered at all?

The further we would get from our apartment in the morning, the more comfortable and calm my mom seemed to get. Early on during the drive in the mornings, she always played the same couple of songs in the car. We'd listen to the Jackson Five's greatest hits as she'd sing the words to each track that she played at a very calm and lovely tone.

She drove with her window up and with a very alert posture. She drove sitting upright with two hands on the steering wheel all the way until we got onto the on ramp for the interstate. It was almost as if my mom was holding her breath until we were in some type of clearing. I never understood what caused that sense of worry or…fear in my mother's heart but it was always something that I noticed.

But on the long car ride to school, my mom made sure that I had either a banana, an apple or a fruit cup to eat for the ride. As we would get further from home and closer to my school, the mood in the car shifted magically every time. My mom changed the music around the same exit on the highway each morning and an indescribable peace came over her. The next couple of songs were by Lauryn Hill who sounded like an angel singing about things that made me feel like she lived in my neighborhood. And every morning

46

before the ride was over, we would listen to one or two of my mom's favorite gospel songs.

As we pulled up to school during those days there was such a huge difference in everything that I saw out the car window. The buildings became houses, lovely, spacious houses that looked like mini mansions. The concrete and cement that I was used to seeing at home turned into fresh green grass that was always perfectly mowed. The street signs were clean and didn't have any graffiti on them or any damages done to the poles that held them up. Instead of homeless people laying on the ground and standing outside of corner stores all day and night, I saw young white women jogging and men in suits walking their dogs to and from really nice dog parks.

But the biggest difference that took place as we left Southeast and made it to Sidwell every morning was the smile on my mom's face at the point of finally getting into the kiss and ride car drop-off line.

While my mom may have felt excited for me that I was going to a school where there wasn't the same type of issues like at my other school, the only things that ever crossed my mind was being able to play for their basketball team. It didn't matter to me if I played on a team in Southeast with Dajuan and my cousins or if I played on the Sidwell team. All that mattered was that one day I'd get a chance to play. Ever since I could remember, my mom wanted me to get really good grades and to be like her. But for reasons that I can't understand, reasons that are buried deep down inside of me, all I wish that I could be allowed to do is *hoop*.

As we made our way back and forth from Southeast to Sidwell, over and over for those two school years, my mom made me feel like I was the smartest kid in the world. She'd ask me really hard math problems on the ride to and from school and she would always ask me about my favorite book that I read from any given week.

To my mom, I was a mini lawyer. I was a mini genius. I was a mini…her. But I wish that was how I felt when I was at school all alone and without her by my side. Most of my memories from being in class at Sidwell were different than what my mom probably thought they were like. Instead of answering all the questions correctly in class the same way that I did during the car rides with her, at school I was barely even called on. Instead, I sat in class as one of the only Black kids in the room, barely ever speaking a word.

A teacher would ask for volunteers and I'd raise my arm and wave my hand like it was on fire. Most of the time, my teachers looked right through me like I was made of glass. And when I did get called on, sometimes kids would laugh or giggle because none of the teachers in the building could ever say my name the right way. Instead of Uh-lee-yuh, they'd called me Ally, or Al-uh. I never really had it in me to correct them, so I just ignored it and tried to do my best to answer the question.

Being at Sidwell made me question what it was that my mom saw in me. I didn't know how to see value in myself or feel good about my life when the people who were supposed to help me never even took the time to learn how to say my name the right way.

But just in case you think that I am exaggerating about feeling left out, think about this for a second. What made things even worse was in the fourth grade when we got ready to learn about Black History Month. I remembered how we only talked about slavery and how we only read a short article about one or two important African Americans. When our teacher showed us a picture of Harriet Tubman, some of the white boys laughed and whispered about how ugly she looked in the photo.

Before I knew it, our unit ended with a short clip of Dr. Martin Luther King Jr. talking to a group of people in a black and white TV clip. We spent the rest of the month celebrating Valentine's Day and something called American Heart Month.

I never really felt like the kids or teachers at Sidwell really liked me and I never found out why. During lunch time and recess while I was there, it just felt easier to sit at the table with the other Black kids. Although I looked like them on the outside, sometimes they didn't like talking to me either. All I know now is that my fourth-grade year was finally over. Unfortunately, if I thought that being at Sidwell was bad, I hadn't seen anything yet.

The summer came and went and only one thing was for sure. Even though My mom loved me with all her heart, it didn't help when it came to needing money to pay for such an expensive school. As the new school year neared, I knew that Sidwell would no longer be the place I called home. So, that August I was nervous and afraid of what was next. My name is Alyah Marie Ramsey and my life was about to get terribly interesting.

Scene 1

During the summer I had seen
Crimes that had all shared a theme
The ones who work to keep us safe
Were taking lives during the day

The TV had displayed a boy
Black and young holding a toy
The cops showed up and suddenly
The boy was killed right on the screen

Nobody knew just how or why
The officer feared for his life
But what was he so scared about?
Checked the boy no weapon found

Every week others had seen
Crimes that simply shouldn't be
What was I supposed to think
When those in charge don't look like me?

My mom explained that it was why
She chose to live the lawyer life
Helping those who need her skills
Protecting lives from those who kill

And then one day it all just clicked
No one on TV would admit
How being Black seemed like a crime
Disregarding lives like mine

People screamed "justice for all"
Racism had been the cause
Tried to figure out just who
Was loved by red, the white and blue

A year ago in school I learned
Of Blacks who worked hard just to earn
A chance to live a life in peace
They took their protest to the streets

Lead by those who knew the truth
Many died in their pursuit
Their fight was worth each life they lost
Social justice at all cost

And then in class we talked about
Amazing people from the south
Men and women, Black and White
Helped the people to unite

They all chose to share the truth
Chose to love, were peaceful too
Confronted those who did the harm
Explained that how they lived was wrong

The year was 1968
A man in charge and he was great
He asked for Civil Rights for all
Jobs and houses, change of laws

He started off describing peace
A life no one had known or seen
At first police had stopped his cause
He didn't quit and so they marched

Dr. King became the man
That many did not understand
How could he be so bold and brave
To fight for justice, unafraid

Gave such an amazing speech
Rights for all he aimed to reach
His dream was full of love and life
What happened next just wasn't right

Someone thought he had to go
They took our King right off his throne
Instead of asking for revenge
The world just wanted hate to end

America had much to change
For years there was just so much pain
Since the start of 50 states
Black people felt tons of hate

So many tried to work it out
And many forced to close their mouths
Continued marching loud to see
A better world to live and dream

And now I'm left to wonder how
The change they wanted comes about
If years ago they fought for us
We must fight and learn to love

Something still gets in the way
It's never flashed before your face
I see it when my mother cries
A pain that's buried deep inside

We saw how life for others is
Peace and wealth, *advantages*
But where we live we all feel bad
We ask for peace, it never lasts

Are we the birds, maybe the cages
We live our lives creating pages
I'm the author and I write
But time will tell how long the fight

If we are trapped and can't break free
We are the birds then, certainly
But if we are what locks us in
We'll figure out just how to win

And if we make it out alive
We'll fly real high and soar the sky
When life begins to show the way
I'll thank the Lord each day and pray

I want to know how it will be
My future holds uncertainty
The gift of life is hard at times
For now we live some *Crunchy Lives*.

Fifth grade began with strange events
Ms. Brown our teacher, came and went
I've had a teacher quit before
My hope in school I can't restore

The last two year I saw just how
A private school supports a child
But now I'm back where I began
Unsatisfied, forced to attend

My school is called EPCS
Elite Public School, I guess
Can't forget it's called a Charter
People think it means we're smarter

But my first month back was bad
Here is how the kids all act
First the boys all call you names
Say mean things right to your face

If you raise your hand to read
Boys make faces you can't see
Talk so bad behind your back
Silent bullies, that's a fact

A girl in class made one mistake
Read a sound the word ain't make
Kids then laughed at her attempt
But I had known just what she meant

I then tried to help her out
Right when I tried, I heard a shout
"Oh you think you really smart?"
Hand on mouth, he faked a fart!

Everyone then laughed aloud
After that I closed my mouth
I was scared to help again
It was the worst way to begin!

The principal sent home a note
Hoping parents don't revolt
She stated that they'll figure out
How best to serve their children now

In the letter she made clear
They'd fix the problems from last year
However, no one knew for sure
Uncertainty we'd all endure

It took my mom all that she had
To comprehend what it all meant
How could another teacher leave?
Removing all stability

The students in my class denied
Ms. Brown a chance to teach in stride
They misbehaved so much in class
Ms. Brown resigned so quick and fast

We only had her for a month
The start of school was far from fun
These boys they laughed and made some jokes
Our teacher quit, her heart, they broke

It took some time to understand
Why kids chose to ignore their chance
In order to succeed in life
We'd need a teacher, smart and bright

Ms. Brown she seemed to fit the mold
But boys acted like 4-year olds
I can't believe they disrespect
Teachers who care and do their best

Before I came back to this school
I learned about a change in rules
Long ago a kid like me
Might just not have learned anything

My old school made it loud and clear
To make the most of learning there
I felt as if I had no choice
To learn the most from every course

The teachers did not seem to show
Interest in how far I'd go
They only mentioned how the times
Now allow a face like mine

Because of that I owe respect
To ancestors who risked their necks
At one point Black people could not
Learn in peace, they would get stopped

So to see the boys act out
Goes against what I'm about
Those before us even died
To risk giving reading a try

I live the way I do from how
My mom makes sure I think about
The key to making it in life
Give thanks to those who sacrificed

I mean, for real...my class is rude
Disrupting school is what they do
My old school taught me so much more
How schools somehow oppress the poor

It's true that once there was no way
For Blacks to learn throughout the day
They were excluded from the truth
That learning helps you make it through

The kids who I now see each day
Think it's a game, they joke and play
They throw away their chance to prove
That they can be successful, too!

I won't give in or be like them
I'll lead and be inspiring
It might not be my role today
But someone has to pave the way

How's my mom taking the news?
We can't move, I can't switch schools
It cost too much and that's just that
I'll have to learn right where I'm at

Ms. Brown did what was best for her
Her leaving us revealed the hurt
The pain that kids like me create
When rude to those who educate

The time between the change in roles
A couple kids had unenrolled
Where they went I have no clue
I doubt they went to better schools

It's just so strange, I'm nervous now
She quit, her bags were carried out
I love school, I thought she knew
She left and gave up on me, too!

Either way my mom's upset
Who in the world will teach us next?
They'll have to be the perfect fit
Or else success it won't exist

Either way we must prepare
For the tests we take each year
It shows that we are capable
And that we're smart and fit the mold

Without a teacher who can help
We'll have to study for ourselves
But some don't have a mom like mine
Who helps with skills and takes the time

We can't feel sorry for ourselves
Hang excuses on a shelf
Time will tell how well we strive
Persisting through may save our lives

Ms. Brown is gone, no coming back
My motivation still intact
Her memory will be erased
Only a star could take her place

Until then we'll wait and see
Who will they find to take her seat?
A man, or woman…possibly
Whoever comes they must believe!

They'll have to know deep down inside
That teaching us begins with pride
They won't support us if they can't
Set the tone well in advance

Scene 2

September ended sad and dark
The next phase was about to start
Brighter than the hottest son
The new teacher, a special one

His visit was the other day
Those violent boys, they came to play
Charles and Jamal, they fought
The new teacher was caught off guard

He saw just what the class was like
Two of the boys had had a fight
I wondered if he'd change his mind
A class like our so far behind

We were told he never taught
An *athlete* from the very start
He only dreamed of teaching kids
Would our class be the perfect fit?

He walked in at the perfect time
Felt just what it would be like
One more week, then he's in charge
To change the class would be so hard

Our principal was sad to see
That kids did not act quite like me
The day that he had saw the fight
I was seated, acting "right"

I did not shout or leave my seat
Hyping a fight wasn't for me
My mother taught me to behave
Use energy to get good grades

When the class came to a halt
Our principal began to talk
"What in the world got into you,
You hit each other here in school?"

Ms. Brown was spending her last day
In tears, no time to celebrate
I wish she had a better time
Her last day ruined, such a crime

Our principal, afraid for sure
Would Mr. Leroy hit the door?
I wonder if he thought to leave
He wasn't phased was what it seemed

Instead of backing down and out
He spoke to us all loud and proud
"'Good afternoon, you boys and girls,
I'm sure you feel like it's a thrill

Yes I once played in the league
A superstar hard to believe
The NFL is in my past
My next job will be in this class

I will be your teacher soon
That's why I'm here this afternoon
I know that we can be the best
Excited for all that comes next

But this behavior has to stop
Next week we'll start right from the top
We'll focus on the basic facts
That I'm in charge and that is that"

He walked away and left the class
We all were shocked and had to ask
If he would really teach us now
We felt so lucky, don't know how?

I wondered the entire day
When I got home, what do I say?
Do I explain just who he was
And he'll take over for us?

Will my mom know who he is?
Or will she have to *google* this?
I hope he ignores what he saw
Did Charles ruin it for all?

His first day in, he saw a fight
I hope he sees I do things right
It won't be fair if I can't learn
Those boys are rude and they take turns

They make fun of all the kids
Take last week for an instance
A girl named Kayla in our class
Smart and sweet but always sad

In class she struggles just to see
They move her seat like every week
Have to find a spot for her
Somewhere close so she can learn

I felt bad knowing her deal
But her sight no one can heal
Spends some time in class with us
Then gets on a special bus

Has a specialist that knows
Ways to teacher her I suppose
And because she has a cane
Kids mistreat her to her face

But each time you hear her talk
See her smile, see her walk
Everyone around can tell
That she's strong and she prevails

I can't see the reasons why
Kids in class, they make her cry
Even though Kayla is blind
Her future will be bright like mine

Still the boys won't let her be
They laugh because Kayla can't see
But even though the girl is blind
She sees more than them all combined

No one has to fight for her
Now the jokes don't even work
Hopefully the boys will learn
Because they sure get on my nerves

Disrupting almost everything
And wonder why they can't achieve
If they would stop, sit still and chill
They may find dreams that they can fill

I pray they learn a lesson soon
But acting bad will be their doom
Mr. Leroy seemed sincere
"Next week, no misbehaving here"

The night before our brand new start
I couldn't sleep, just turned and tossed
I tossed and turned and did not sleep
Imagining such pleasant things

Our class would be the best of all
A new teacher, famous and tall
I didn't know what to expect
Just hoped that I would benefit

My mother woke me up in time
She made me eggs, I loved them fried
She made some pancakes, soft and gold
Drank some juice and hit the road

We pulled up to the school to see
A big ole' truck with TV screens
A man and woman standing proud
Tons of fans watched from a crowd

The news had spread so quick and fast
A famous man would teach our class
It was really happening
I couldn't wait…I had to scream

My mom, she kissed me on the cheek
She said to have a perfect week
Got out the car, I strolled on in
walked up to class, proud to begin

I walked into the same ole' room
Something was new...a different tune
It felt as if we all had been
Freed from fear from deep within

We did some things to break the ice
We all had fun, it felt so right
But Charles was still down and out
He found out he lost recess now

Thought Mr. Leroy would forget
To punish him for what he did
One thing that we learned right away
Our new teacher, he doesn't play

Don't put his patience to the test
He does exactly what he says
We threw away all we had done
A brand-new unit just begun

When times were tough we had the help
But have to want it for yourself
No one will make you try your best
In our new class we'd all have tests

One thing that would come about
Nothing bad came from his mouth
Made us feel that we could win
We learned to try from deep within

Mr. Leroy…now you know
He'll care for plants until they grow
And when we all get stuck below
The pruning starts, promptly but slow

He showed us that there's several ways
Persist, endure, don't be afraid
When your turn comes let it out
Have pride to answer, time to sprout!

Although I see my cup half full
A couple kids can't even pour
They made a mess and dried it up
For them they'd wish for better luck

Because back when they were friends
A superhero had walked in
Some say bad luck some say poor them
I say it's dumb what Charles did

He struggled to control himself
Got mad and swung, he needs some help
Too bad because this guy's so great
And Charles can't relive that day

Charles started off all wrong
Missed recess for God knows how long
I knew just how things would go
Our new teacher, professional

Accountability would shape
All that we'd grow to love and face
This year I'll learn more than just facts
Detention! I'm avoiding that!

As days went on we'd leave our cage
Exploring topics, proud and brave
We thought about Ms. Brown for sure
But this new journey--safe, secure

It wasn't wrong, it was just right
Our lessons seemed to all align
A greater purpose, more to see
We learned about our history

Mr. Leroy said a lot
Managed to get the boys to stop
Sometimes they still caused a stir
But usually they did their work

He asked us things like no one else
Made sure we saw things for ourselves
Didn't just tell us how to think
Allowed for kids to be unique

"Which way to go, who should you trust
Ignore the news, see through the fuss
It's fine to question if unsure
The cage is open, do explore!"

October was so reassuring
School could sure be full of learning
We saw the passion in his eyes
Our teacher yes…one of a kind!

Scene 3

The first attempt he set the bar
Not too high and not too far
He introduced a topic that
Brought our imagination back

"So who can tell me who they are?
Describe with details, every part
I want to know just what's inside
Are you brave or are you shy?

If I can't get a volunteer
I'll go first so all come near
My name's Tyrone and once I played
With kids and they were twice my age

But growing up the way I did
I challenged all the older kids
I was so fast, and I was strong
Until a bully came along

He told me that my skills were wack
I asked him if that was a fact?
We didn't fight, we simply raced
I put that bully in his place

From then on the kids all knew
That Tyrone Leroy was the TRUTH
As I grew my skills improved
Known as the best athlete in school

So right around 11th grade
Every college knew my name
Recruited by the best around
I represented for my town!

Became an All-American
Kept working hard to benefit
Capital Academy
Helped me to fulfil my dreams"

"Mr. Leroy can I ask…
Why'd you quit if you're so fast?
If you're the man, then why are you…
A teacher here with us at school?

Why give up the joy and fame
And leave the crowds that cheered your name
How come you quit so you can teach?
I don't get you, honestly"

"All good points you mentioned there
In time I'm sure that I will share
But for now listen and learn
Teaching is now my new concern

I hope that I am crystal clear
We've much to do to fix this year
You lost some time messing around
But you'll succeed and here is how

I know that there's a big state test
Don't worry, that we will not stress
Instead we will go down a path
You'll learn and you'll enjoy the tasks

Open your notes and listen close
This will keep you on your toes
I explained just who I am
Now it's my turn to understand

Write about just who you are
Your dreams, your goals, and all your flaws
When that is done we'll move along
What's next is learning where you're from"

Mr. Leroy had me think
About just who I want to be
I wrote it down and wrote a bunch
Excited to share after lunch

On our way down to the cafe
I couldn't wait, I had to ask
"Mr. Leroy do you think
That girls can hoop or do we stink?"

He looked at me with great big eyes
His words they caught me by surprise
"You are Alyah, aren't you?
At recess how about we shoot.

I'm guessing that you like to play
Is basketball your favorite game?
If so, just know I think that's great
My dream and yours they both relate"

I can't believe he answered me
My teacher, a celebrity
He told me if I liked to ball
That I should shoot hoops all day long

During recess we both played
He helped me shoot, improved my game
The boys, they all had seen me shoot
My teacher then nick-named me "**Hoops**".

From then on, the name, it stuck
Amazing! Can't believe my luck
This year will surely be the best
Our new teacher will fix the mess

During that week we all received
Assignments that we loved to see
The task required much of us
A different tone…a voice to trust

Our teacher introduced a man
Most people in the world were fans
But what we all just read and saw
Was knowledge that you can't ignore

Back in 1492
A crew had sailed the ocean blue
And when explorers saw the land
We thought they loved Americans

But at that moment we all learned
He harmed the natives, slash and burn
The crew they came took all their gold
And forced them all to hit the road

Now this is different, yes, I know
Columbus Day is wonderful
A holiday to honor him
But now we should get rid of it

There's more to life, as kids we're blind
These new facts opened my eyes
In class we took the blinders off
For years our history was wrong

I couldn't wait to make it home
I questioned if my mom had known
Me excited makes her feel
She mastered all her parent skills

During the next several weeks
Things calmed down and class was sweet
Back and forth to home and school
Was smoother than it was before

We learned and built skills as a class
The year began to move real fast
October flew by like a bird
But one kid still got on our nerves

His name was Charles that I knew
Called him Crunchy, hard to chew
It's almost like he can't behave
He gets in trouble everyday!

Crunchy couldn't get it right
Rude and always tried to fight
I saw him stay behind in class
To vent, to share feelings he had

What most kids got excited for
My classmate Crunchy, he ignored
October 31st was here
But he was sad from ear to ear

My mother taught me to avoid
From worrying about the boys
But something crazy deep inside
Made me feel sad for Crunchy's life

That day in school was full of fun
Candy passed to everyone
But when I looked around to see
We missed Crunchy from the scene

The classes got to march around
With costumes and our bags were brown
I saw a group of kids miss out
Sat in the office, heads were down

I guess you get what you deserve
If rude in class and you don't learn
Our teacher is the best around
He never yells and always smiles

Mr. Leroy motivates
He makes me want to be so great
The boys find ways to mess it up
Miss out on trips and other stuff

If I were them, I would behave
Wouldn't want to have bad grades
The end of fall is when we sort
Who's allowed to hit the **court**

Basketball's about to start
I love the game with all my heart
I know the boys will want to play
So I hope that they all behave

And from what I hear from them
I'm sure they hope to see the gym
But all I know is I'll be fine
Can't wait to join this team of mine

I'll be the best one on the floor
All of the kids will watch me score
Of course, I'll pass and play some D
But my name's Hoops so watch me lead

One thing that I've never shared
Unsure if my mom would care
Winter meant it's time to ball
But no one knows, no one at all

I want my mom to know the truth
My dream of dreams is just to hoop
I practice when she's not around
Ten-years old, the best in town

During November break I watched
The NBA and couldn't talk
My mom don't want me wasting time
The law's her dream but hooping's mine

I'm scared to open up and say
That her dreams will not work for me
If ever I can tell the truth
She'll see my skills and love them, too

Maybe I could get someone else
To tell my mom just how I felt
A person who she'd listen to
Here's what they'd say, only the truth!

"A doctor, lawyer then retire?
But a warrior's insider her
Jordan, Kobe, Lebron James
Mind is set to add her name

A list of greats she reads each day
Basketball she yearns to play
Dribble, pass, shoot and score
The crowd she hears them shout for more"

        But what is all this silliness?
        Her mom won't let this dream exists.
        If it were up to her alone
        The courthouse is what she'd call home

        They are loved and needed most
        But scoring points beats saving folks
        To her she sees no other way
        She hides her fear and plays her game

Can it be that passion dies?
Competing with the older guys
Aspiring to be the best
In P.E class she says "I'm next"

Stepping on the court is sacred
Boys won't let her ever make it
Known as Hoops with Nike kicks
She plays and skills are evident

Magically she darts and dashes
Scoring threes and flawless passes
Where did she get strength to play?
Her mother, yeah well…certainly.

When Ms. Ramsey was her age
She played and played with tons of rage
But that one day back in her teens
A violent thing, horrific scene

Her brother was the best in town
But kids made sure they'd lay him down
One bad day at seventeen
Ruined young Ms. Ramsey's dream

Her brother shot and killed that day
Then she was never the same
Instead she vowed to make it *out*
A doctor or a lawyer route

So naturally that's what she wants
Her daughter's life…escape from thugs
She's never let Alyah play
The world she knows won't ever change

Scene 4

Things in school were going well
I loved our class, bet you can tell
And just when things were going fine
My slip, my mom refused to sign

The day she came to pick me up
Under my arm, my ball was tucked
I dribbled walking to the car
She knew her *no* had left a scar

"Hey baby, how was school today?"
"We read, and wrote and laughed and played"
"That's nice, it seems like you're just fine…"
"I'm not, I'm sad about my life"

"Wait a minute, girl what's wrong?
Did someone hurt you? Do you harm?"
"That someone's not a kid at all
I'm sad that you won't let me ball"

"You need to focus on your grades
Don't worry 'bout playing games"
"But I am good, the best in school
They call me "Hoops" they think I'm cool

"That's not your name so cut it out
You'll be a lawyer, make me proud!"
"That isn't what I want to do
My mind is set on college hoops

Becoming pro will follow that
I'll use my fame and I'll give back
With being on the tv screen
I'll help more girls follow their dreams"

"That sounds so nice but give it up
You'll be a lawyer, girl just trust
I'm your mom and I know best
You'll thank me later on for this"

November quickly came around
And life was moving faster now
The holidays were coming up
And tryouts left Alyah stuck

She had to find a way to play
And somewhere after school to stay
She lied and told her mom that she
Had extra credit to complete

But one thing that Alyah missed
A team for girls did not exist
She realized and she almost cried
Should she pretend to be a guy?

Her only way to join the team
She'd have to make them all believe
That she was not a she at all
Here goes nothing watch *him* ball

The next few days were really strange
Alyah asked her mom for braids
Her hair was easy to point out
She had to style it different now

"So, baby why the change in style
Your long hair seemed to flow for miles
Did a kid say something mean?
Your old style was a style for queens"

"No one is mean, I just want change
I think I'll like my shorter braids
My long hair, it got in the way
And when I read, it's in my face"

My mom did not seem curious
Blending in is serious
When try outs start back up next week
I'll change my voice and talk *real* deep

I hate that it's the only way
Why won't they allow girls to play
I heard the teachers loud and clear
My only option was to *cheer*

Who do these teachers think they are?
My name is Hoops, the superstar
When it's time to make the team
They'll pick the boy who's really me

And once they know I'm good enough
I'll lose the braids and show my puffs
My hair will then show them it's me
And then they'll keep me on their team

But what if my plan doesn't work
If I can't play, I'll be so hurt
Before I put my plan in play
I'll see just what the coach will say

"Coach Williams, hey…good afternoon
I know that basketball starts soon
I heard this girl who's in our class
Compared to her, the boys are *trash"*

"Hello, Alyah…how are you
I heard you like it here at school
A girl who's better than the boys
I doubt that's true, sound like some noise"

"What do you mean, you doubt it's true
I saw her play, I watched her shoot
No boys could stop her or get close
Regarding points, she scores the most"

"Well if she wants to make my team
I'm sorry but that cannot be
The rules for now won't let her join
For now, my team's only for boys

It's not my choice, it's just the league
If she's that good, she'll wait and see
I wish there was more I could do
Because I'd love to change the rule"

I got my answer, now I know
I'll put my plan in motion slow
I have my braids, I'll squint my eyes
I'll change my look, be in disguise

My mom, she doesn't seem to know
That to the gym is where I go
If one day she finds out I lied
I'd break her heart; I know she'd cry

I shouldn't have to make this choice
The team should not just be for boys
And hopefully when they see me
They're let some other girls compete!

I had to let it go for now
We're on our break, family in town
My mom cooked an amazing meal
Thanksgiving time is such a thrill

To some it's just another day
For my family we eat and pray
We're thankful for so many things
Could always be worse than it seems

School includes some holidays
But all don't seem to feel the same
I love what comes from family
But some would swap reality

My cousins came from deep down south
A few of them sleep on the couch
The ones who get to use the bed
Are crazy packed, sleep feet to head

The grownups laugh and reminisce
They speak of those they love and miss
Remembering when they were kids
They seemed to live for times like this

My mom she bragged about my grades
They seemed so proud and even prayed
I heard that other kids my age
Were not just quite doing the same

"Well…my son can't get it right
Seems like he fights all day and night
I know his daddy ain't around
But that don't call for actin' out"

"We have to do the best we can
Our kids are smart and understand
That when they get to be our age
They can't live life with all that rage"

My relatives were really cool
Better than the boys at school
They didn't treat me wrong at all
And asked if I liked basketball

I got excited, suddenly
I chose to tell them everything
We talked about our favorite teams
They mentioned so much more than me

They asked what playing meant to me
And who I wished that I could be
I realized that they knew a lot
Started explaining from the top

"Alright, Alyah check this out
We play all day down in the south
Our favorite players aren't guys
That you'd probably recognize"

"Okay, so tell me who they are
I'll add to what I know so far
I guess they played back in the day
So, go ahead and please explain"

"Many fans don't even know
He joined the league and stole the show
The year was 1981
And his career had just begun

Drafted as the 2nd pick
Soon after that his name would stick
He was an all-star through and through
Isaiah Thomas was the truth!

But right around Isaiah's prime
Another player comes to mind
It led to some fantastic games
But dude straight up just took the fame

Some say he's the best of all
Was legendary with the ball
Most people know of his shoes
But on the court, he could not lose

They say that he became the *GOAT*
Was he the best, well…we think so
Michael Jordan, flying high
Won 6 rings, can't be denied

But these two players made it hard
They did not let him take it all
Before MJ became the MAN
Magic and Bird had all the fans

Larry Bird was also great
Played his best in 88'
Boston Celtics was his team
Should be top 15, at the least

The other guy who also reigned
Made it hard for Mike to play
Magic Johnson was his name
Flashy passes changed the game

The greats who played around that time
Played their hearts out every night
The NBA just ain't the same
Probably the best when they all played

Talent didn't stop with them
They paved the way for more to win
Magic passed the torch to Mike
Then Mike had tried to hold it tight

Then there came another guy
Was young and had just learned to drive
He didn't go to college like
Thomas, Bird, Magic or Mike

He hit the scene creating sparks
Lakers gave the kid his start
Wasn't long til' he became
The best to ever play the game

It didn't happen right away
Jordan tried to make him pay
The decade ended with a bang
Kobe Bryant won his ring!

Mike and Kobe were the Kings
Combined they won 11 rings
Six for Mike, he leads them all
The two of them, they set the bar

That brings us up to recent times
This next player's hard to describe
Like Kobe he entered the league
By skipping playing college teams

Lebron the King is who he is
He's strong, he's fast, and very big
I never seen a guy like him
He soars and flies above the rim

Although he's only won three rings
His greatness never goes unseen
Captivating every crowd
His family is extremely proud

What makes him cool is how he helps
He spreads the love and also wealth
He built a school and he gives back
There's nothing that his greatness lacks"

"Wow, y'all seem to know a lot
Keep going, what else-please don't stop
I want to learn about them all
When I grow up, I'll also ball

For now, my school won't let me join
The team they say is just for boys
I have to figure out a way
To prove to them that girls can play"

"That sucks but, tell us…what's your plan
Just sneak on-act like one of them
It's easy to dress like a guy
No make-up and just squint your eyes

You shouldn't have to hide your face
But wear a headband just in case
And if they make you take it off
Talk real deep instead of soft"

Thanksgiving helped in many ways
My cousins knew just what to say
My mom enjoyed the company
We didn't want our fam to leave

Scene 5

But time had passed, December's here
Not a great part of the year
We moved on and our class learned more
Poetry's what we'd explored

Mr. Leroy talked about
Healing using words out loud
He mentioned people that have done
Poems that helped saved more than one

I never once imagined ways
How poetry can heal our pains
As people we all come to know
That life alone is miserable

The poems we read all made it seem
That living was their favorite thing
Langston Hughes was Black and proud
Ms. Angelou ignited crowds

They mentioned how the country should
Be better than it ever could
And one thing that I learned for sure
Was poetry that open doors

The tasks before the winter starts
Was to write right from the heart
Kids shared thoughts and said some themes
But I could not choose anything

It was the first of times that I
Had something troubling on my mind
Distracted by reality
I'd have to lie to make the *team*

It was finally the time
I pushed back my pick up ride
The school day ended, right on track
And basketball season was back

Dismissal came and students left
Tryouts today would be my test
I changed my gear and got in line
I warmed up in the gym with pride

My headband helped cover my bangs
I used a deep voice it was strange
I had a fake permission slip
If I get caught, my butt is whipped

I didn't care and did not blink
I knew that all my shots I'd sink
I ran and ran and ran some more
I played D and no one scored

They cheered me on, encouraged me
But who I was they could not see
The team was only meant for boys
A girl was best, made all the noise

At the end the coaches said
They'd let us know who'd represent
Told us they'll post names for sure
My *best* I left it on the court

I checked the clock and it was time
My mom already parked outside
The place she knew or thought I'd be
Not the gym, the library!

I grabbed my bag and hit the door
Out of breath and very sore
I had to act as if I was
Reading, not betraying trust

I changed my shoes and switched my clothes
If I'm slick she'll never know
The library is where I went
Not sure I can do this again

"Hey, Alyah…there you are
Let's go let's take this to the car
How was staying after school?
Extra credit…that's so cool"

"Yea, I mean it was alright
Had to read, take notes and write
I think that there will be more days
To stay after and raise my grade"

"Oh, okay I see that's fine
Just let me know, I'll be your ride
I'm glad that you still study hard
Your success, it warms my heart"

Days blew by like fallen flakes
All unique in their own way
The fifth-grade class received a treat
A fieldtrip made for royalty

Mr. Leroy pulled some strings
His kids from class could not believe
They just traveled in limousines
Were chaperoned up to their suite

Once all at the stadium
Mr. Leroy welcomed them
"Hello, class…now this is cool
Far more fun than when at school"

Almost all the crew was there
Alyah, Kelvin and Jahir,
Jadah, Leah, even Steph
Crunchy and Mike the ones they left

He still acted out at times
Missed out on the special ride
Some may say that wasn't fair
But Crunchy was still acting weird

Jamal had been invited too
The kids all seen his grades improve
They wished Crunchy had followed rules
Maybe he would once back to school

So back to what our teacher did
He got tickets for all the kids
Even let our parents come
A football game, just tons of fun

We sat where famous people did
Announcer even mentioned it
"Good evening everyone out there
Special guests are standing near"

He welcomed the entire class
My head was spinning super-fast
I looked up on the jumbo screen
And standing there was only me

I waved and jumped and grabbed my mom
The camera captured everyone
Before the end we had a chance
To go downstairs right to the fence

The players came and touched my hand
I love sports, its biggest fan
Maybe this will show my mom
That sports can impact everyone

My mom took pictures in her phone
After the game we headed home
I looked through all the ones she took
New memories now in my book

Before Christmas Break

Our teacher is the best of all
Here's one thing that's helped for sure
He took us all to see a game
Amazing time, we felt the fame

He took us all in limousines
We ate for free and loved the scenes
But not all kids came on the trip
Crunchy and Mike, missed all of it

They didn't do their jobs in class
And missed a trip from acting bad
I felt sorry for them both
Hope they learned their lesson, though

And at the game my hunger grew
Now I really want to hoop!
I'll work until my dreams are real
But have to help my mother heal

She doesn't know I know her story
Heard her pray one day for glory
She had said, "Lord, heal my heart
Lost my brother at the park

And Lord please keep Alyah safe
She's talented and wants to play
But going down that road won't work
My heart can't take the pain, it hurts"

I understand why mom's afraid
But one day soon she'll see me play
I'll ask her to come to the gym
She'll see me score on all of them

The basketball season is here
And Christmas time is also near
December is a crazy month
Santa, gifts and lots of fun

The new year might just be the day
That my mom just lets me play
I'm still unable to express
I love b-ball and am the best

At school, they think she signed me up
If she finds out, she'll whip my butt
If news gets out, she'll want me done
Except my journey's just begun

Think about taking a ride
A roller coaster, fast and high
With tons of flips and awkward turns
No time to think, emotions blurred

At first, it's fun, exciting, screams
But then you fear, it shakes your knees
As if you wouldn't make it out
The kinda' ride I'm talkin' bout'

That's sort of what the winter's like
I pray that Santa's on my side
My mom, she does the best she can
But we're alone no helping hand

Our ups and downs are painful when
We think how Santa won't come in
Christmas just reminds us that
My dad moved on, no coming back

When other families get to love
My mom just prays to up above
We know life could always be worst
But why can't God just put us first?

Winter was in full effect
Cold as ice, cover your neck
My cousins didn't make the trip
The snow had kept them where they live

Every year we get a tree
A tiny one, the size of me
And each year when I make a list
I pray my mom gets most of it

So, this Christmas just me and mom
She took some time off from her job
The holiday would be my chance
Defend my point, explain my stance

I tried to find the perfect time
To tell her of this plan of mine
But every time I thought to talk
She gave me chores to get crossed off

I made the floors all squeaky clean
My mom made me scrub everything
From counter tops and under rugs
I cleaned til' there was no more dusts

When I got tired and upset
My mom pitched in to clean the rest
And once we both were done for sure
She changed my mood, made bubbles soar

We laughed and played with soap and suds
Her love had spread and by the tons
She told me thanks for all my help
Could not imagine someone else

My mom, my hero, my best friend
We got each other til' the end
We watched some movies through the night
Just one day left til' Christmas time

Scene 6

I fell asleep right on the couch
When I woke up the lights were out
I walked around and it was strange
Nothing there seemed quite the same

I looked for something that I knew
But life was different, magical
I walked quiet like a mouse
A kingdom had replaced our house

I shook my head in disbelief
"Was it really happening?"
My legs were mine, and arms…the same
I shouted out my mother's name

The castle that replaced my house
Put me in shock, hands on my mouth
Looked out the window just to check
The scenery, magnificent!

I checked to see if I was real
Pinched my cheek, I tried to feel
I couldn't seem to understand
I heard a sound and then I ran

I tried to find a place to hide
Instead I darted right outside
This had to be a dream of mine
The snow reached up into the sky

I looked around and all I saw
Was beauty here and near and far
Shinny crystals, fancy ice
This couldn't possibly be life

Moments ago, my mom and I
Were on the couch, just closed our eyes
For Christmas Eve we cleaned the house
But words for this just won't come out

I tried to call my mom again
Heard nothing good, only the wind
I turned around, my house was gone
Became afraid, what's goin' on?

I screamed out loud for someone's help
Down from the snow, there fell an elf
Stuck in my tracks I couldn't move
I said "this is impossible"

How in the world could all this be?
This isn't real, I'm clearly sleep
Wake up, girl...I told myself
Maybe the elf was here to help

I had no choice I said hello
He looked, he hopped and then he spoke
"My name is Sizz and I'm your guide
No need to run, no need to hide

You may not realize where you are
We're in your town, we aren't far
But what we see if different from
All you know and all you've done

Snapped his fingers, just like that
A magic sled appeared from scratch
He told me what would happen now
We'd see some magic in the clouds

"You need some help from up above
Taking a trip so buckle up"
That's when my confusion grew
Where'd he want to take me to?

Got on the sled, nothing to lose
Unsure why I'm who he would choose
The sled began to slowly float
High in the sky is where we'd go

There were no doors, just comfy seats
The elf made sure his sled was neat
He clapped his hands and we were off
Snow was blowing, felt the frost

As we got further from the ground
Couldn't believe what else I found
The snow was not the best of scenes
Above the clouds the world was green

The freezing cold had gone away
The elf confused me with his sleigh
I thought we'd head to somewhere cold
This new place though, was wonderful

The sun was out, and clouds were blue
I saw some red and purple too
Even orange, maybe pink…
I had no words and couldn't think

The sun was warm and sparkled bright
A waterfall was to my right
Palm trees, they were everywhere
I couldn't help to smile and stare

Were we in Heaven, possibly?
Rainbows, they were all I seen
He dropped me off and waved goodbye
I felt abandoned in the sky

"When you're ready shout my name
I'll bring you home, the way we came
But do explore and figure out
What's here for you above the clouds"

Unsure if this was real of fake
I shook my head and made my way
I walked along a yellow road
The scenery was beautiful

As I walked, I seen a lot
White flowers with purple dots
Golden birds and lovely trees
Shades of blue and gorgeous leaves

Nature was amazing here
No pollution, skies were clear
I kept on going and I seen
Clear blue water in the stream

I stopped to look and as I stared
A pretty older face appeared
I smiled and she smiled back
A lovely face, nothing she lacked

The water rippled suddenly
The face I could no longer see
I walked along the road again
Trying hard to comprehend

The place was great, but I was lost
I walked up to a bridge to cross
On my side it was so nice
But over there what would I find?

Already in over my head
I chose to cross and move ahead
As I stepped, I felt the breeze
Birds were singing in the tress

Moments passed and I felt safe
A woman was soon in my face
"Hello, dear…you made it up
Now take my hand I'm fine to trust

You may not know who I am
But trust me, I'm your biggest fan
We never had a chance to meet
But know that we are family"

Her smile I had recognized
She knew my name I was surprised
What did she mean "my biggest fan?"
This dream I still don't understand

"Yes, that was me in the stream
You're safe with me, just watch and see
You have a secret, I'm aware
Partly why you're now up here"

The lady took me by the hand
We talked and walked and talked again
I listened well to all her thoughts
She had one huge amazing heart

She told me that I could achieve
Everything I'd want to be
However, she made sure to say
She wants me to live honestly

I guess she knew about the team
She must know things about my dream
"One day you'll be a superstar
But tell your mom or break her heart

You have to tell her how you feel
With mothers lies are hard to hear
If she finds out about your lie
You'll shatter all her trust inside

So, listen as I tell you this
These words of mine, do not dismiss
And when it feels just right to do
Tell my daughter "mom loves you"

I stepped away from being shocked
The information rocked my block
The woman who had been so kind
Had been a grandmother of mine

As soon as she said her last word
She disappeared; existence blurred
I huffed and puffed and searched around
My grandmother could not be found

The sun began to fade and set
I realized that I had to jet
I called for Sizz and he appeared
He greeted me and saw my tears

"I guess you found out why you came
We can't leave yet, there's one more thing
Your grandma is so kind and sweet
She left you one more special treat

We have to go back to the stream
To make a wish and then you'll see
Just what else that there is for you
You do this task and then you're through

We headed over to the stream
The water still peaceful and clean
I had no clue what wish to make
All I could do was breathe and wait

Suddenly the wind picked up
Trees began to sway so much
The leaves, they started falling down
Birds were flying, soaring round

Deep inside I felt a tug
Soft but pure, was just enough
I dropped down to my knees and prayed
All confusion went away

I closed my eyes and said aloud
I want to make my mother proud
And just like that the wind, it stopped
Bubbles floated to the top

I reach into the stream to find
A tiny treasure chest inside
I held the box up close to see
The gift inside was all for me

As I opened up the chest
I closed my eyes and held my breath
A brilliant light was trapped inside
Golden hoops were the surprise

"Oh, my goodness those are nice
I can't believe what was inside
Put them on, they're yours to keep
They're perfect and they're so unique

One last thing, this time I swear
This final thing I have to share
Your earrings, they are powerful
Here's a rule you'll need to know

If you lie to anyone you won't achieve your dream
If you break the only rule, then you will not succeed
If you lose one of the hoops the power won't exist
Understand you need them both to have any success"

The moment came for us to leave
We headed down below the green
Sizz was now taking me home
My mom I had left all alone

I got dropped off right in the front
Sizz took off and wished me luck
I walked back in and then I saw
The night was right where I left off

My mom was sleeping on the couch
The TV on, the movie loud
I turned it off and went to sleep
Still unsure about the dream

Hours later we woke up
I got my mom her coffee cup
Hot and black like every time
The special morning started fine

"Merry Christmas, to my queen
You make me smile, my everything
Thank you for the special card
Your love made it into my heart"

"Mom, I love you, that's a fact
You know I'll always have your back
I made that card just so you know
My love for you is magical"

"Alyah, what are on your ears?
Where are those from, who brought those here?
I never seen those things before
Are you sure that they are yours?"

"Mom, what are you talkin' bout?
I'm confused, I'm missing out"
I reached up to feel on my ear
Golden hoops were sitting there

"Oh, my goodness what are these?
Mom were these a special treat?
You put them on when I was sleep
They're so nice, they can't be cheap"

"No, I didn't buy you those
Where are they from, girl I don't know"
"Okay, you can stop joking now
If you got them, I'll figure out"

"I'm serious I have no clue
But girl, them *thangs* are beautiful
Not sure where you have found them at
So maybe we should give them back?"

"But give them back, wait back to who?
They just appeared right out the blue
Can I wear them, pretty please?
They look so great, perfect for me"

My mom she let me keep them on
We sang all day, just Christmas songs
Through the day she gave me gifts
One at a time, right off my list

The day was perfect, certainly
But something strange was on the tree
I went over to check it out
My chin had nearly hit the ground

Suddenly I recognized
The object in front of my eyes
The memories of meeting Sizz
Had come back how could I forget?

I thought that I had had a dream
Was it real, it couldn't be?
The hoops that I had in my ear
Remembered how I got them' there

I traveled to a magic place
A special land I thought was fake
But if none of the trip was real
How do I have these earrings still?

I was shocked and couldn't move
My mom started to notice too
She called me once, she called me twice
The third time looked me in my eyes

"Girl, what's gotten into you?
I called you twice, you didn't move
Our day was long, for sure…indeed
So maybe you should get some sleep"

I listened to my mom's advice
I hit my room and closed my eyes
I couldn't sleep all I could do
Was think about the secret rule

"If you lie to anyone you won't achieve your dream
If you break the only rule, then you will not succeed
If you lose one of the hoops the power won't exist
Understand you need them both to have any success"

The next few days were full of stress
I couldn't choose what to do next
When we go back to school next week
I'm sure they'll add me to the team

But if I lie and break the rule
My lifelong dreams, they won't come true
I contemplated what to say
The truth will be the only way

Scene 7

January 1st was here
What better way to start a year?
I set my clock to talk to her
But my mom seemed so very hurt

"Good morning mom, are you okay?
I noticed you don't look so great
Is there something I can do?
If so, just know I'm here for you"

"Morning baby, no I'm fine
I get like this, like every time
I called your dad, no answer there
I feel like he don't even care

Your father should have wrote to say
He hopes you're happy and you're safe
But that is far from what he did
And that...I just cannot forgive"

Because of what my mom went through
I chose to wait to tell the truth
Time flew by and just like that
Our break was over, school was back

This year 5th grade moved so fast
Christmas break ain't really last
Now we're in the 2nd quarter
Grades are strong, always in order

I have to focus on these tests
The road to greatness starts with it
Tons pressure on my shoulders
Mom works doubles, that's what molds us

I never talk about my dad
He doesn't help and never has
Does he love me, I don't know?
His heart is caged, the key is broke

In time I'm sure my mom will say
The reasons why he went away
For now, I listen, and I pray
I hear a whisper, soft and safe

It tells me that I'm great and loved
Don't fear, your life will be all good
I never ask what voice it is
My heart it knows, those words are his

We've never gone to see his face
The memories of him erased
My mom tells me she sends him pics
I am his pride she's sure of it

Maybe I get my skills from him
Maybe he's like Kobe and them
If it is true, then let me be
I'll do my best, the MVP

The more I learn the more I see
Men like my dad the world mistreats
Maybe he did have tons of flaws
Ten years alone, not fair at all

Problems comes when dads are gone
Most kids I know only have moms
Can't learn it all without a man
We need help from the other hand

I saw the news, it made me cry
A boy my age…shot down…he died
He was alone no dad around
I felt so bad, tears on the ground

I guess that's why my mom sees life
Me as a lawyer, only right
She wants me to grow up and serve
To be a voice for the unheard

That way black kids who live will know
Their lawyer loves them, heart and soul
But If I do all that I can
By hooping I'll encourage fans

Then black boys and girls will see
Instead of hate, they can achieve
Either way I'll help them out
They'll live their dreams, make families proud

Several ways I can support
I'll soar the skies, on every court
When I make it to the pro's
Girls will love how high I rose…

Like a flower in the street
They'll believe because they'll see
A warrior, a queen for sure
A little girl who opened doors

And grew so strong and never quit
Then they'll have hope, a bunch of it
For now, my mom still calls the shots
She's my queen, all that I've got

My teacher made that loud and clear
That he, my mom and family care
I've always viewed my life as blessed
But Mr. Leroy gives new tests

He makes us question all we've seen
My growth, my mind, exceeds my dreams
What once was just a thought of mine
Is real, I've left my fear behind

At ten years old I'm brilliant, bright
Still a kid in mommy's eyes
If she only knew my thoughts
She may just give me grown-up job

For now, I'll chill and play it slow
I'm Hoops, I play, I pick and roll.
Gotta tell her who I am
Basketball, its biggest fan

For me it's more than scoring points
Leave life to chance, like flipping coins
For us it lands on tails a lot
For kids like me the dreaming stops

My mom, she fears like I will break
But I build strength all through the day
I grow strong from watching her
That's how I know, my dream will work

When I can't improve outside
I dribble in my room at night
My mom she hears the bouncing noise
And takes the ball, my heart destroyed

This life I live is all day long
I can't improve because my mom
I don't care if she can't sleep
I need my skills to be unique

When she's not here, away at work
I sneak around, I search, I lurk
I find the spot she hid my jewel
I grab my ball and off to school

The new year would require me
To start the year with honesty
I went to school wearing my hoops
Reminded me just what to do

January meant that we
Would see who made it on the team
During the day the words came out
My plan had helped me beat the doubt

Posted clear for all to see
Eleven names, including me
Me, but really not Just I
I made the team in my disguise

Today my thought was to come clean
Before I seen I made the team
And now all that I want to do
Is disguise so I can hoop

If I want to live my dreams
I'll have to tell them that it's me
What if they don't believe that I
Am actually the headband guy?

Or maybe I don't have to say
I just won't show up on the days
Then that way I can still remove
Myself from staying after school

Something still feels like it's off
The truth is I'd still have to talk
And let my mom know what I did
I'll Tell the truth and all of it

I made sure to communicate
No extra credit for today
My mom picked me up at the bell
Was nervous and my fear was real

We drove home but we cruised a bit
No rush at all was evident
My mom turned on the radio
The DJ then started their show

"Good afternoon all of my folks
Here's something that you need to know
January is the month
That we shout out all those we love

We'd like to take a second and
Congratulate a special friend
Viola Ramsey, proud and strong
A mother and a lawyer, y'all!

She graduated at the top
Howard U…and she don't stop
She fights for all who need a voice
We love you girl, keep making noise!"

The DJ said amazing things
Great that it was happening
My mother's spirit lifted high
She looked so proud and so was I

As we made it the house
My words I planned would not come out
We made it all the way inside
Through dinner and then through the night

I can't believe I froze again
Imagining her listening
What she would say, how she'd react
Not sure why I kept holding back

I guess I just could not allow
Anyone to slow me down
I'd miss out on the fun from ball
And none of it was fair at all

How could they not allow the girls?
To show off their amazing skills
What if it wasn't only me?
I thought of all the other queens

I wanted to stand up for them
Not just I, we all would win
Remembering the radio
"Fight for those who need you too"

That week I found the time to ask
I shared all of the plans I had
I told my mom about the team
The *headband boy* and everything

She punished me for just a week
Not allowed to join the team
I was upset but felt relieved
She learned to put her trust in me

Now that the pressure was removed
I could focus back on school
Mr. Leroy told us all
About a fieldtrip we'd go on

Before we'd get prepared to leave
We learned about society
The new unit was *Government*
We studied laws and politics

We started with the fight between
A country and a greedy king
He wanted all the land and fame
His ships found land they tried to claim

"Alright, class so listen up
We've been learning tons of stuff
And with our field trip coming up
We'll be prepared for what's to come

Let's pick back up from what I taught
We'll learn about how countries fought
In England we know that a King
Had tried to conquer everything

Great Britain sent some boats across
Own the country was their cause
Natives fought but they all failed
And colonies tried to prevail

England reigned and set up shops
The colonists asked them to stop
At first, they played and got along
But then somehow all things went wrong

Before our country got its name
The land was used in many ways
Native people far and wide
Lived on the land with tons of pride

But people from far over seas
Came to explore and they believed
That whatever they walked across
Belonged to them but they were wrong"

"So, Mr. Leroy, can I ask
Why would the King treat Natives bad?
It doesn't sound like it was right
Did Natives try to stay and fight?"

"Your question leaves me to believe
That you see how wrong this could be
But during times back from the start
Great Britain tried to make its mark

Before the 50 states we have
The King treated the Natives bad
The Natives had their land replaced
With colonies, their lives erased

That brings us to a point in time
Where no one stopped to see the line
The line that Europeans crossed
America was the result

The British King was challenged by
A leader who England despised
The man who I am speaking of
A general, who rose above

George Washington became the man
The president, governed the land
There was a shift and power changed
The country was then rearranged

The 13 colonies became
The 50 states and changed their name
With all the changes that occurred
They needed rules for it to work"

And because of all of this
A holiday came to exist
The fireworks that you all watch
July the 4th is why they're sparked!

"Oh, I get it, I see now
The country changed, they worked it out
The King was not the one in charge
A President replaced that part

Then the groups were not a team
George Washington changed everything
The colonies were then combined
The government helped them unit

We celebrate the holiday
So, the date don't fade away
I get it now, it all makes sense
George Washington, 1st President!"

"That's when the men who ran the show
Came up with branches you should know
Legislative is the team
That makes the laws we're following

They include the Congress who
Includes the *House* and *Senate,* too
Judicial Branch is who is next
This is where the laws get checked

This group includes the many courts
Commit a crime, go through these doors
Now this one is so powerful
Of course, you need the others, though

However, listen very close
It's the one you know the most
Executive means *President*
The White House, where they work and live

Presidents, they carry out
What other branches talk about
You combine them just to see
How structured governments can be"

We finished work and took a break
We learned so much in just one day
But as I thought about it more
Came up with thoughts we should explore

Scene 8

Before the day came to an end
I raised my hand and I began
"Mr. Leroy, please explain
From forty-four I saw one name

One Black face and that was it
The rest were all White Presidents
How come there weren't any more?
Was it a law or something or…?"

I'm sure he knew I was sincere
Not being rude, I showed I cared
And at that point he took a seat
Reassured it wasn't me

He said that it's the reason why
He quit the league and said goodbye
No longer cared about a sport
Wants kids like me to question more

"Well why do you feel that there is
A lack of men who represent
Not that there aren't ones who tried
But their voices have been denied

But what makes our country great
Is how even through all the hate
Black men have never quit or said
That they can't be our president

Obama was the first to win
But there are tons with confidence
Sometimes their efforts go unseen
But don't let that disrupt your dreams"

Dismissal time had come again
I put my reading in the bin
Pushed my chair beneath my seat
Mom had pulled up to wait for me

January would involve
A trip that changed the world we saw
The plan was to go on a tour
Georgetown is where we'd explore

I had known about the school
That made my mom so very cool
But this old University
Was not a place I'd ever seen

"Okay class, today we'll learn
Of colleges you may have heard
In case they may be new to you
Take some notes, that's fine to do"

Going on a college trip
Was helping us with confidence
Mr. Leroy had his ways
Wanted us to turn out great

"Alright, college is the place
You go after your high school days
Most people finish up in four
Some stay longer to explore

If you go and do your best
You'll graduate and you'll be blessed
Then you choose a great career
But that isn't our focus here

Colleges are great because
You learn so much from everyone
Faculty will help you out
But you make friends that last a while

Here are some you need to know
If you believe, then you can go
Columbia, UPenn, and Brown
Are awesome schools so write them down

Vanderbilt and MIT
Are also great, that's true indeed
There's Harvard and there's NYU
They're all fantastic schools to choose

Yale is great, imagine that
One of the best, and that's a fact
Put it on the list for sure
And UVA…of course there's more

But down the road in your own town
Is the school we'll learn about
Georgetown Hoyas is the team
Grey and blue, a perfect scene"

Mr. Leroy made it clear
That college was nothing to fear
He made sure we all took some notes
In case we questioned where to go

But one school that he didn't say
Is where I'd love to hoop some day
One day at home watching TV
It showed the UCONN women's team

Their team had set the bar so high
So many wins, I thought they lied
The truth is that they were the best
Plenty records that they set

At some point I am sure that I
Will talk to him about my life
I'll mention how I plan to be
On the UCONN women's team

The day had finally arrived
My mom was coming for the ride
She loved the thought of college trips
And knows we're not too young for them

The bus pulled up and we got on
The ride was short, ain't take that long
We took the route to get there quick
Screams, the bus was full of it

"Settle down, you're all too loud
Please, I need you to calm down
When we get up to the place
Stay in your seat until it's safe"

The bus had parked, and it was clear
The students, they must love it here
Fancy building, lovely bricks
I sure did not imagine this

When we got into the hall
Were not allowed to travel far
Had to stick with the adults
Place so big you could get lost

"Alright class, now listen up
Our food is here, stays on the bus
There are things we have to do
Here is your guide, he welcomes you"

"Hey fifth-grade, I'm glad you came
I'm your guide and Sean's my names
I attend the school of law
Whoa, you're taller than I thought

Sorry, that caught me off guard
Anyways, the tour will start
First, we'll head to see the cafe
Then the science buildings last

As we make our way around
Notice it's like our own town
Here, we have all that we need
Place is great, just follow me"

While other kids were making jokes
In my head I took some notes
I noticed in some of the rooms
People studied, some in groups

We walked some more and then we saw
Flat TVs against the wall
Technology was everywhere
So many tools, no need to share

We made a stop and met a man
He said he studied in Japan
Then came back to campus here
Foreign student for a year

Amazing life after 12th grade
My mind was blown, I was amazed
My mom, she saw me smiling when
A girl walked by, looked like my twin

She had on clothes that made me ask
Grey and blue and Nike Tags
Her bag was huge, like a balloon
The girl was off to practice soon

"Hey, look mom, does she play hoops?"
"I think she might, she probably do"
"Can I ask or please can you?"
"Yes, I will, I'll ask real soon"

My mom walked over to the girl
Tapped her and then she stood still
Smiling and they both shook hands
Heard my mom say, "she's a fan"

That's when they both walked to me
Got excited, couldn't breathe
As she stood in front of me
Had to look high up to see

"Hey, girl, oh those hoops are cute
They look perfect on you, boo!"
"Yes, these things are powerful
Came from somewhere magical"

"If you say so, guess that's cool
My name's Coral, who are you?"
"I'm Alyah, glad you stopped
This lady, well she's my mom

Had her stop you just to see
If you play basketball like me?
If you do what is it like?
I'd love to learn about your life"

"Heard you were intelligent
Try to make the most of it
Back when I was just a kid
I helped my mom when she was sick

Because of that I'll be nurse
I'll graduate, go right to work
Yes, I do play on the team
Studied hard, followed my dream

Not sure if people tell you this
Brains and balling co-exists
Stay focused on both for sure
Then success will be all yours!"

"Mom tells me to study law
She won't let me play basketball
Team at school is just for boys
Can't wait til' when it's is all my choice

"Alyah, now you know the rules
Laser focused when at school
Besides, just like I said before
You'll be a lawyer, girl of course"

"Hey, can I just share a thought?
My captain also knows a lot
She's an All-American
And studies law, she just began

My point is that you can do both
No disrespect, but I think so
Started young, built confidence
Achieving goals, I'm evidence

Either way, you both are great
Please enjoy the tour today
If you ever have the time
Come on and watch a game of mine"

Ms. Ramsey was upset
Said some things she would regret
Had the chance to open up
Should have shown her daughter love

Scene 9

The group continued on their tour
They took some pictures and explored
Mr. Leroy got in line
But no one knew the reason why

He spoke to the security
No one heard no one could see
He came back and he told the group
Something special they could do

Mr. Leroy's eyes were wide
Addressed his class with tons of pride
He cleared his throat, began to say
"Michelle Obama's on the way!"

"Michelle Obama, who is that?"
Shouted out a voice from back
The group all turned and were surprised
Could not believe she was inside

She came to speak to college kids
But somehow they got on the list
The group would get a chance to see
A lady, brilliant as can be!

Mr. Leroy made it known
Mrs. Obama held the thrown
Married to a president
First Lady is what he meant

Alyah and her mom were shocked
Their differences they had forgot
Soon they'd get a chance to meet
A hero they'd both like to be

Before the class could come inside
Security gave reasons why
Reasons why they'd get removed
If they were loud if they were rude

The host had mentioned why she came
Not at all because of fame
The school was honoring a month
A month the First Lady has loved

As the kids all took their seats
The monitor began to speak
"Today we have a special guest
Deserving of so much respect

Without any more delay
Clap your hands along with me"
After all the cheering stopped
The First Lady was on the clock

She only had a little time
To share all that was on her mind
"Greetings every one of you
I'm so glad you're in the room

I want to take the time to say
We're all unique in our own ways
Each of you is beautiful
And life has much in store for you

I'm here to launch a special month
A month that's filled with so much love
Peace and positivity
A time to display unity

My college journey all began
Back before Barack had ran
Although the White House was our home
There was a time I was alone

A young Black girl with plans and goals
I wasn't sure which dream to hold
All I did was concentrate
I didn't quit I didn't break

When things got hard and weren't right
I thought of those who sacrificed
They worked real hard just like a team
And many died so I can dream

Now that it's me who's sitting here
Which one of you will conquer fear?
Who in the crowd has dreams like mine?
If you believe, you'll be just fine

We honor those who paved the way
And celebrate their legacy
It isn't over, wait and watch
Achieve your dreams and don't you stop"

The crowd all stood up on their feet
Amazing words, still can't believe
Our trip became the best of all
The First Lady put us in awe!

"We only have time for a few
Maybe 3, but really two
Are there any questions here?
We'll take a volunteer from there!"

As I sat still in the crowd
A shinny light was on me now
Was it really happening?
I'd get a chance to ask some things?

I couldn't move, started to shake
The whole moment had all seemed fake
My mother nudged me, and I said
"Can I have a hug instead?"

The crowd erupted in a cheer
They loved my thought, sweet and sincere
Security all looked around
Michelle had made her way on down

Everyone stood to their feet
She got close enough to see
My legs both shook and arms were weak
She hugged me and then touched my cheek

The fieldtrip was my favorite day
Nothing else that I could say
Got on the bus and closed my eyes
Imagined I was soaring high

As I floated in the clouds
My view was nice as I looked down
Tons of possibilities
So many things I could achieve

I scanned the earth from mountain tops
Swaying high no plans to stop
Breathing deeply just to know
A life like that was possible

The bus returned us to the school
Best trip ever, super cool
Mr. Leroy made it known
He loved our school and headed home

I couldn't wait to see what's next
Our memories, hard to forget
My mom had even said that I
Brought tears of joy to both her eyes

Scene 10

February here and proud
I love my skin I say it loud
Black and precious as can be
We learn of heroes every week

One day I argued with the best
Today Kelvin made me upset
He joked about the way I walked
I joked back, he made me fall

My mother raised me to behave
I'll have to find a slicker way
I think to challenge him to race
I'll beat him, put him in his place

Kelvin is competitive
But so am I, Hoops always wins!
We line it up and then we're off
Lose to a girl, and he'll look soft

I leave him in a trail of dust
"You cheated, girl, rematch, we must!"
But time is up, I got revenge
He's laughed at now by all his friends

But back to class now let us see
We read and write, so brilliantly
It's time for social studies now
We learn of things from all around

So first we hear about a war
An evil man, hateful for sure
He killed so many lovely folks
The reasons why? I still don't know

But what we learned hurt deep inside
How I felt, I could not hide
I asked what countries fought him back
Our teacher mentioned who attacked

America came to their aid
They sent the troops and joined brigades
Life for the world, not peaceful then
But World War II came to an end!

Shifted to read about a man
Who lived during that same time span
Earned gold medals, ran real fast
Who was he, I had to ask?

You got my attention now
Impressed the world, not just the crowd!
The first to ever run a race
The world at war and full of hate

Racism did not stop his drive
He braved the danger, did not hide
A hero he became to all
Jesse ran so I can ball

Mr. Leroy lets us know
A project is what he has shown
Choose a figure from the past
Who helped improve the lives for Blacks!

The timeline is all up to you
But just be sure you see it through
If this gets tough, just ask for help
But try to do it by yourself

When at home I'll share the facts
I'll say how I want to give back
The dream I have growing inside
I'll stand for change like *Owen's* life

Jesse's life will help explain
How athletes can help pave the way
Around the world moms need to know
Sports stars all have hearts of Gold

But sometimes my mom makes me feel
That I can't add value until
I decide to follow her
A female doctor or lawyer

"Alyah, girl…your mother's home!
Your teacher called me on my phone.
He said that you are doing fine.
You make me proud, you child of mine!"

"Oh, hey mom…okay that's cool.
Here's my new project from school.
It says to find someone who's great
Can't think of someone who relates"

"Directions said, go home and ask
Someone for help, like mom or dad
So here it is, please help me find
A role model, who made some strides"

"Give me a sec, I'll help with that
My first thought, there's so much respect
She was a lawyer true indeed
But she was first for all to see

Her name of course Charlotte E. Ray
Howard University
She argued in the highest court
All of us, she did it for!

You see, Charlotte was powerful
Her role is truly magical
She set the stage for many more
And argued in the Supreme Court"

"Mom, that's great just not what I...
Want to do but I will try...
To find someone that's just like her
But someone that I would prefer"

"Okay then so let's try again
How about a doctor then?
Rebecca Lee is who she was
Last name Crumpler, heart was tough

She stood up to the world and said
I will study medicine
She wrote books and sacrificed
So much time, saved tons of lives"

"Oh, mom here you go again
Not another doctor, man
I want to research someone else
That when I read, I see myself"

"Girl, you know I want you to,
Follow your dreams, I know you'll do
But you're so much don't let it waste
I have to watch the steps you take"

"I know you want the best for me
But I am wise, one day you'll see
Success is something that I'll have
I want to use my gifts from dad!"

"Oh basketball, oh no...child please,
Let me explain who else I see
You can study Ida. B
She opened doors for journaling!"

"At least you'd travel just like sports
Around the world, so many doors
She fought for all our people when
People like her was killed for it"

"Yes, she was fearless and brave
But that's still not my type of game
I want to give back, certainly
A voice through sports, do you hear me?"

My mom made points but I'm unsure
Today in class I'll search some more
But before I could learn again
The boys, they made fun of my friend

As we all worked so hard in class
A note, I saw that Crunchy Passed
Mr. Leroy saw it, too
Had Kelvin read it... "Awwww shoot"

"Well, well, well…what have we hear?
A letter, or a note? Oh, dear!
I don't allow such type of things
Now hand it over right to me"

The boys were caught, they were so rude
Rude to my friend right in our room
I wonder what the note had said
Too late, Riley put down her head

She knew that it had mentioned her…
A joke, some words…I'm so disturbed
Later the boys apologized
But not before tears swelled her eyes

I knew I had to fight for her
But not with blows, just words for sure
During lunch time later on
I faced the boys for they were wrong

I learned through gossip what they said
They laughed at the hair on her head
I took the time to talk about
A millionaire born in the south

Madam C.J Walker was
A brilliant one who helped our cause
See, black girl hair, it ain't no joke
Make fun of us…oh no you don't

Her invention helped us out
But natural hair we love no doubt
Instead of saying something mean
Be polite and love your queens!

I set them straight now back to work
We had some time for one more search
My mom, she mentioned Ida B.
And what I found was great to see

She was for sure before her time
Writing about all types of crimes
Even though there were no phones
She captured mistreatment of folks

Today people…well they can film
What's done that harms and hurt and kills
But back in 1899
Ms. Wells, she wrote between the lines

She interviewed and searched around
Told stories for the Blacks and Browns
Hatred hid what few had saw
Ida B. took blinders off

Because of what she shared in life
The laws were changed to make it right
Although we still have much to fix
She started strong; I'll finish it!

Scene 11

The next few weeks we learned so much
But the boys, were hard to trust
They kept on making fun of things
This next joke, boy…you won't believe

"Okay, class…now who is this?
It's someone that…well…here's a hint
She was a nurse and helped so much
First black woman to do such"

Shouting out, stomping the ground
Crunchy's comment made me frown
He said the woman on the screen
Was ugly and the boys agreed

In my mind I thought just why
He carried on, I was surprised
Crunchy said that she's too dark
His attitude had broke my heart

Why do the boys not see the pain?
How being mean makes kids feel shame
The woman our teacher displayed
Resembled our entire grade

The point is that we don't believe
That Black and beauty is a thing
How can we learn how to achieve?
Have to love yourself, at least?

Mr. Leroy did not shout
Wasn't angry, wasn't loud
In the softest voice I've heard
He simply said "we're worthier"

"Worthier" of more respect
Worthiness we should protect
Learn to love just who you are
And never feel you're less than stars"

So, he explained just who she was
Nurse Mahoney, greatest cause…
She stood for more than health and meds
The first black nurse, she represents!

"Okay, Class…that's it for now
Your hard work has made me proud
Finish up so we can see
What we have learned from HISTORY

My favorite month was winding down
My mom's best friend was now in town
She always came to celebrate
Another year of living great

For dinner we all sat and laughed
They talked of times from in their past
Mentioning how far they've come
Sharing success of her son

"Michael wants to study law
He's smart, and nice and oh, so tall
Argues that he wants to "hoop"
A life like that I can't compute"

"Oh, well I am doing that
Won't take the doctor-lawyer track
I'll change the world by modeling
Girls who "hoop" pursue their dreams

And once I make it to the top
I'll fight for equal rights non-stop
The platform that I can create
Can make the world a better place"

"Aw, Alyah…that's so cute
But put your pretty face to use
Study law, or medicine
Leave playing ball and sports to men!

Ladies like your mom and I
Don't waste our time to be like guys
You only get one life to live
Trust me, make the most of it

Oh, and one more thing for sure
Can't change the world by playing sports
Don't know exactly what you heard
To change the world, you have to serve

To do that you'll have to be
Smart and use your skills to lead
Drop the ball, your dreams no good
I hope my words are understood"

I never felt so hurt inside
A pain like that I can't describe
My mom sat still and did not speak
She watched her friend just crush my dream

But that won't stop me, watch and see
The sports world will make me their queen
And when I make it all the way
I'll make sure that she's at my game

Her and my mom don't understand
I'll "hoop" and turn them into fans
Only then they'll see just why
A caged bird, teaching girls to fly!

After dinner things got worse
"No doctor? Okay, be a nurse"
She kept on telling me to be
Things that were not in my dream

We switched subjects so quick and smooth
My mom knew she ruined my mood
She asked about the kids in class
If I had friends, if I was sad

I mentioned that they did not see
How mean they were to kids like me
I told her that they say bad things
Treat me like you won't believe

I'm smart and nice but in the end
They never treat me like a friend
I only wish kids recognized
Their own pain buried deep inside

And not to mention just last week
They had my friend cry in her seat
Passed a note, cruel as a can be
So what, that she's darker than me

They act like they hate that we're Black
But Black is beauty, that's a fact
I might be *lighter* than some folks
But skin is no reason to joke

From what I know it's all the same
I'm Black, you're Black, just different shades
I'm light, you're dark but we are one
Have to unite for peace to come

But then just right after I shared
My mother's friend seemed unaware
She told me that I'm better off
My lighter skin, problems it solves

She carried on about a myth
That light skinned folks have benefits
She told me not to be so mad
She said I'm lucky so relax

That's when my mom had stepped on it
Put her foot down, and began
Told her friend that she's wrong
Skin makes all blacks not belong

If we will ever get it right
Light, or brown or dark, Unite!
That is sure the only way
We must combine to pave the way

Race can go misunderstood
But when we love, our lives are good
So my mom made sure I knew
That **shades** of Black are beautiful

"You're right, I meant no disrespect
I just want you to be your best
We women have a lot to prove
Only want what's best for you

Whether you play ball or teach
As long as you give everything
Because of those who fought for us
We give our best when times are tough"

"I thank you for your words, for sure
I take advice, please give me more
However please do understand
I'm basketball's most loving fan"

The night came to a peaceful end
My mom, she thanked her trustful friend
But something rattled deep inside
I felt the poking of my pride

Most young girls would disagree
But what she said encouraged me
It showed that if I will win
Not everyone will comprehend

The next few days I practiced more
Being the best was what's in store
I dribbled almost everywhere
On the porch and on the stairs

Failing to eat I watched the greats
I carved NBA on my plate
My mashed potatoes served to show
How focused I was, in my zone

And when I wasn't watching sports
I dreamed of playing on the courts
With tons of fans, shouting so proud
My tears of joy hitting the ground

But back to school so here we go
My favorite month comes to a close
We're almost finished with our task
Only a few more things to add

Before we start the work today
Mr. Leroy came to say
That he watched the All-Star Game
Wondered if we did the same

At first, I didn't think to share
That I knew all that happened there
Of course, I watched the whole event
But should I even say I did?

The boys began to shout and talk
What they had saw, and what they thought
I couldn't help to think to add
That their opinions were so bad

The players that they thought were good
Were not where my opinions stood
But if I add my thoughts to this
My words may just not quite exist

I chose to give my best attempt
To share my knowledge, here it is
Raised my hand, forgot to breathe
And just like that I took the lead

As nervous as I thought I was
I shared my views, received applause
Mr. Leroy heard me say
Some points that only players make

He noticed that I understood
How defense makes a player good
I didn't talk about the dunks
I only mentioned plays that stunk

We both agreed that players need
To sacrifice more for their team
I guess that all the boys now knew
They had a "Hooper" in their school

After that cool morning talk
The time to learn was on the clock
We turned the page and saw a text
A hero from the past was next

Mr. Leroy asked the group
If any of us really knew
How long ago there was divide
How Blacks were not allowed inside

Within our class we learned a lot
We found out how division stopped
It wasn't perfect right away
He challenged the law everyday

The paragraph we had to read
Started off with "who knows me?"
It was a guy holding a bat
Number 42 and fast

The picture showed him and his team
The only Black, chasing his dream
At that point I recognized
Who he was and how he strived!

A man named Jackie comes to mind
He ran from base to base with pride
He could have passed up every chance
But gave Black players legs to stand

The year was 1946
Just days before he broke the fence
The country seemed to make it clear
That his kind was not welcomed there

That did not make him quit the game
Instead he fought and overcame
While most would never understand
United some Americans

In 1947 when
The Brooklyn Dodgers let him in
He could have stopped and given up
But he dreamed for all of us

Without the brave, the Black and proud
We'd all be left out in the crowd
But due to what he added then
My love for sports grows deep within

I wish my mom knew all about
How sports can make her very proud
Of who I want to be and why
An advocate for all Black lives

Will she be proud? We'll have to see
Until then I just disagree
That only doctors can provide
A healing to these broken lives

But back to paying my support
To those who saved us through their sport
I'll learn about the other guys
Who sacrificed their lives for mine!

Without him we'd be left behind
Chasing dreams without a ride
He helped to open many doors
And after Robinson came more!

Black History will be the theme
All month we learned about a dream
Dr. King was brave for sure
But who is that who soared and scored?

I learned about a man name Russ (Bill Russell)
He played in Boston, was so tough
They loved him on the court for sure
But in the world, he was ignored

A Black man, tall and oh so proud
He faced the hate, embraced the crowd
In a time when white men ruled
His hook shot seemed to be what cured

He did not fight, he used his brain
Used basketball to heal the pain
I learned how when he left the league
He made sure other Blacks were free!

Scene 12

The month was almost over with
We learned so much, built confidence
And just when we thought we were done
The real learning had just begun

In the car we heard the news
A superstar with stuff to prove
A quarterback who led his team
But ended up kicked out the league

My mom turned up the radio
More to the story, maybe so
It said that he had took a knee
And took a stand against police

The message also shared a thought
From people who had also saw
Kaepernick had lost his job
From protesting abuse from cops

The world had seemed to make a point
That Kaepernick betrayed the sport
People missed the point he made
He kneeled for Black lives to be safe

How was it that I understood?
But grownups missed his point was good
I quickly thought to share the facts
Might help to bring them up in class

I'm sure that Mr. Leroy knew
My mom said him and Kap were cool
It seemed to be a bigger deal
But as a kid I couldn't tell

February 28th
My class had been my favorite place
I learned about amazing things
But today had felt so strange

In the middle of the day
Kid's began to misbehave
It was so weird, it made no sense
The chaos made me reminisce

Remembered how the boys would act
Felt like Ms. Brown had come back
It wasn't disrespect at all
Someone had shared what they had saw

Our principal had come around
She heard the news, began to shout
At that point I was now aware
Something big had happened here

All the kids were told to sit
The loudspeaker had mentioned it
We sat and waited for the news
What we were told could not be true

Kaepernick was at our school!
Kaepernick was at our school!
Kaepernick was at our school!
Kaepernick was at our school!

Mr. Leroy heard us shout
Puckered his lips, covered his mouth
The face he made; I knew he knew
Now that he's here, what do we do?

We had read about the past
Had learned of those who paved the tracks
Men and women sacrificed
What Kap had did, it felt so right

Mr. Leroy then announced
Something great came out his mouth
"Class we all have to line up
Kap is here, because of us

We will get to meet him soon
Grab your essays from our room
Black Lives Matter is his theme
Equal rights is what he dreams

In a second you will see
The power of you kings and queens
The TV crews will all be here
Not for Kap, for you they'll cheer

One thing that you have to know
Your words have been so powerful
I have shared with everyone
All the great work you have done!"

We grabbed our essays, went outside
The kids from class were full of pride
All the kids, including me
Got close to Kap, it was a treat

TV crews began to roll
The whole school now had lost control
Everyone was shouting loud
Loved the moment, every ounce

"EPCS is the school
There new teacher, pretty cool
Tyrone Leroy used to be
A player on a football team

No longer playing in the pro's
He teaches now, so honorable
And today his friend is here
Kaepernick, let's give them cheers!"

The news reporter finished up
We all took pictures, wished him luck
Kaepernick and his big fro
Hugged our teacher, called him *Bro*

And before we went inside
Crunchy got the best surprise
The last reporter got to see
Him and Kap both take a knee

Mr. Leroy took a pic
Crunchy felt magnificent
He said be sure to cherish this
Black Lives Matter, evidence!

Alyah's Birthday Month

March is here! March is here!
Said it twice for all to hear
There isn't another month
Where I get to have so much fun

Definitely took some time
For the hype to all subside
That means that it took a while
For things to finally calm down

January was insane
Got to meet, oh…what's her name?
Sike, I'm kidding you know who
The First Lady was beautiful

Just when we thought things were great
Kap came to help celebrate
We had made it on the news
Our lives matter, that we proved

Now we are finally here
I smile from ear to ear
I will get to celebrate
My birthday comes up on the 8th

Hopefully the weather's nice
I'd love to celebrate outside
But there is one thing to do
State test prep is coming soon

Before the new unit began
The boys were back to being friends
It took them months to hash it out
Jamal was cool with Crunchy now

When our teacher started off
He saw the boys all acting rough
They huffed and puffed and finally fought
Mr. Leroy saw it all

But now they seemed to get along
I'm glad, the class is wonderful
It means that I should get to see
Quiet time and have some peace

Although our teacher does his job
When boys argue they're really loud
So now that they all worked it out
They'll be no one to scream and shout

Safe to say that we were fine
Mr. Leroy eased our minds
Told us that the tests were near
But not think about that here

Instead we focused on the tasks
Another project here alas
Time to get back in the books
Still so much misunderstood

"Morning, class…How's everyone?
Today we'll have a little fun
I have some coins placed in my hand
Who thinks that they know this man?"

Mr. Leroy had his ways
To get most of us engaged
But this lesson he began
Started off with coins in hand

I took one look and quickly knew
A big ole' face, ain't need a clue
On the quarter we all saw
Washington's ole' face for sure

Then our teacher turned around
Took out a coin, all small and brown
Raised my hand to answer him
But another kid began

"Oh, I think his name is Abe
My mom said he freed the slaves
Don't know the date or when it was
But I know him, he fought for us"

"Abe Lincoln, you answered right
Fought for peace during his time
We will learn about the rest
But for now, know Abe's the best"

During class we read a bunch
Saw some words that tripped me up
Emancipation was the first
As we moved on it just got worse

Mr. Leroy challenged us
I didn't yell, I didn't fuss
It actually excited me
Because I get to learn new things

During the week we moved along
Learned of how the country fought
Lincoln was the President
But the country almost split

The South wanted to have the rights
To own slaves and run their lives
The North had different feelings, though
They thought slaves should be let go

As we learned it added up
Honest Abe, someone to trust
He signed important documents
Now that big long word made sense

Emancipation Proclamation
Switched the way he ran the nation
It allowed for folks to start
Helping Blacks to make their mark

Tons of others helped the cause
Many names, the list is large
Nat Turner known for his heart
His bravery had left a mark

Before they ended slavery
He risked his life to break them free
Tubman, Truth and Rosa Parks
All helped the cause, they played their part

Mr. Leroy gave us time
We learned of all who helped define
What our country came to be
Without them, doubt that we'd be free

Nowadays class moves so fast
Already time for P.E class
At home I never get to shoot
Can only dribble, have no hoop

My mom had told me I can't play
But during gym, I have my way
Fifty minutes to myself
I pretend I'm somewhere else

"Starting in the All-Star Game
Saving lives with tons of fame
Wearing fancy golden hoops
Give it up, our girl can shoot!

She's from D.C and plays the best
Alyah…wins and doesn't miss
She also has a charity
Helps the homeless eat and sleep!"

When I make it to the pro's
That's how my intros will go
But for now, in P.E class
I shoot and work on how to pass

One more day before the 8th
My birthday and I cannot wait
But today in class with me
Kelvin must want to get beat!

He takes my ball and runs around
Stops and shoves me to the ground
I never push him back at all
Instead we just play basketball

He doesn't know I practice, too
I dribble better and can shoot
Now the class is watching us
Cross him up, oh yeah…I must

"Alright, man…you think you're good?
Mess with me, you think you could?
Mr. Leroy calls me hoops,
Earned the name from how I shoot!"

At that point I dribbled right
Stutter stepped and he lost sight
Kelvin was left in my dust
Scored so easy, class went nuts!

Beat him bad, scored easily
Scored again and shot a three
After that it got so bad
He then started talking trash

"Girl, you think you big and bad?
You ain't score, I gave you that
Wait til' it's my ball again"
"Boy, stop with your arguing"

In the end I showed him up
Made it clear that girls are tough
Said somehow I cheated him
Could not believe a girl could win

After gym we went to eat
But someone said the boys were mean
I wasn't sure who said it first
But someone made my day the worst!

"Alyah is really a boy"
I heard that and I felt destroyed
Why would kids make fun of me?
I'm respectful and so sweet

"She beat Kelvin one on one
Only boys can get that done
So next time y'all see her play
Call her *boy*, right to her face"

I was crushed and couldn't breathe
Why would kids say that to me?
I didn't know just how to act
I ate and cried, went back to class

I put my face down at my desk
Mr. Leroy could not guess
Asked the class to please explain
No one mentioned Kelvin's name

"Someone here needs to speak up
I don't condone this type of stuff!
If someone here is being mean
After school you'll all see me!"

At that point that's all he had said
Let me relax to rest my head
But before I could say a thing
Crunchy walked right up to me

"Alyah, hey are you okay?
I saw what people said today
Sometimes people say mean things
But it's because *they* are hurting

My mom tells me not to fear
It's hard to do, but ugh…for real
I think you're smart and good at hoops
Don't worry what they say to you"

That was the second time all year
Somebody told me not to fear
It helped to hear somebody say
"Ignore the boys and jokes they make"

Scene 13

The day was over I went home
I went right up straight to my room
Slammed the door and took a seat
My mom came up to comfort me

"Alyah, baby…what is wrong?
In the car you didn't talk
Got home, ran up and slammed the door
Something's on your mind for sure!"

I almost failed to answer her
She wouldn't get why I was hurt
Should I mention basketball?
Won't understand my pain at all

"The boys, they're mean they call me names
It started when I chose to play
I beat a kid and they all saw
At first they cheered, at least I thought

But during lunch somebody said
I'm not a girl, a boy instead
And that's when everybody laughed
I then put my head down in class

Mr. Leroy tried to help
He noticed I was not myself
But as the class came to an end
Someone helped me, he's a friend"

"Aw, Alyah, girl don't cry
Kids are mean, I don't know why
But trust me when I tell you this
You are a queen and don't forget

And also God knows who you are
He made us all, unique at heart
So when somebody bothers you
Like me, you're tough, you're bullet proof"

My mother made me feel alright
But something still was off inside
She hugged me and that's when she saw
A hoop of mine had fallen off

It must have happened when we played
I didn't feel it fall away
The earring was a piece of me
Its power gone, so is my dream

I thought back to that crazy time
When I went on that magic ride
The words that stuck with me that day
Was a message to obey

"If you lose one of the hoops
The power won't exist
Understand you need them both
To have any success"

I can't believe I lost my hoop
Wasn't sure just what to do
If it's true what Sizz had said
My dreams in life are now all dead!

I jumped up and I wasn't sure
Tell her what the hoops were for?
Did it sound like make believe?
And what would she then think of me?

Instead I chose the silent route
Didn't scream and didn't pout
Thought of plans to search around
Man, where can my hoop be found?

March began, I fell behind
Wasn't what I had in mind
The first week was not great at all
Lost my earring playing ball

I tried ignoring all the grief
Thought today I'd feel relief
This only happens once a year
My birthday and I couldn't care

"Good morning Princess, look at you
Have a perfect day at school
See you quarter after one
I'll bring treats and have some fun"

"Thank you, mom that sounds so great
No one could ever take your place
But what I'd want the most today
Is us to hit a court and play

Maybe if we shoot around
You'll see what makes me happy now
I want to hoop and that is why
I once had dressed up like a guy

What I really need from you
Is your permission, let me hoop!
Every spring teams reappear
AAU season is near!"

"Alyah, now I know you think
Me stopping you is being mean
But really you are unaware
Of how sports really interfere

My brother who had lost his life
Was playing ball, just with some guys
Then there came a tragic scene
Someone shot, took him from me!

Don't think that it would happen twice
But follow me, and live your life
You can become all that you dream
But you and ball, don't work for me"

"But mom, what if it leads the way
What if through sports I demonstrate
A life of service that provides
Hope and faith for many lives?"

"I know your heart just wants to help
For now, worry about yourself
You are young, eleven now
Let's get to school and make me proud"

The day began so plain and stale
My special day, no one could tell
Our reading block came to an end
Then Mr. Leroy mentioned it

"Class, hey so…who filled theirs out?
Y'all do know what I'm talkin' bout?
No one knew just what he meant
Then Crunchy shouted that he did

"Yeah, for sure, I finished mine
I do one every single time
I never guess the winners though
But yours will probably be close"

What was Crunchy mentioning?
My mind was blank, I couldn't think
He then put on a highlight *and
March Madness*, it just began

He cut off all the light in class
All I saw were dunks and flash
College teams, only the best
Thirty-two would start a quest

Something I had never seen
So many amazing teams
The highlights helped to fuel my drive
And then that's when I closed my eyes

The competition would include
Only one important rule
If you lose your season's done
An undefeated champion

I sat as my excitement climbed
The tournament, one of a kind
In my mind I saw a scene
With me playing right on a team

My jersey, red and white and gray
From the crowd, my mom would wave
Then just as the game began
My mom had knocked and came right in

"Good afternoon Miss, how are you?
So glad you made it up to school
For a break we watched a clip
College hoops, magnificent"

"Oh, that's nice, good afternoon
Hello class, I come too soon?
I'm came to celebrate today
My daughter's birthday, on the 8th!"

"No, you're fine your right on time
Hey, Kelvin can you hit the light?
If you want, please take a seat
I'll go get plates so they can eat"

Mr. Leroy was so nice
He had great manners, so polite
Made sure that my mom felt fine
She had come sooner than the time

Passed out cupcakes to the class
Girls were first and boys were last
Crunchy wasn't here today
Wished I could have saved his plate

Before the celebration wrapped
My mom went over and she asked
Something that I couldn't hear
Mr. Leroy seemed to care

Whatever she had said to him
Made me feel something deep within
I hope she didn't talk about
The day from when my hoop fell out

Don't want my teacher to believe
That I complain from everything
I'm big now and yes I'm for sure
Not her *baby* anymore

Still can't find that hoop of mine
The next few weeks I failed to try
Gave up looking, dreams declined
I guess my mom was right this time

Basketball dreams gone astray
But I won't get carried away
Some might say I shouldn't care
But not when life don't seem so fair

Although it was hard to relate
Mr. Leroy mentioned games
Said March Madness was intense
But I was missing all of it

Decided to give it a break
Only focused on my grades
I didn't feel the joy inside
Without hoops, not much to life

The project we received for spring
Required me to make a scene
I had to write a script or play
Had to act it out some way

I partnered with another girl
Her life was different than my world
While I complained of missing ball
Her life was harder, couldn't *walk*

Her name was Maya, short and sweet
To work together we switched seats
We had to be close to the board
The project had us moving more

So when we needed more supplies
I got them for us, didn't mind
Working with her was unique
The way she smiled made me see

That confidence comes from within
Maya was my new best friend
She worked so hard and did a lot
We got an A right on the spot!

Time to present what we made
Maya, man…my friend was brave
As she rolled up to the front
Locked her wheelchair to stand up

She had braces on her legs
They were there to keep her straight
But before she started off
Kelvin laughed, he faked cough

I knew what he tried to do
Interrupting, oh so rude!
No one seemed to notice him
Brushed it off and we began

"Imagine flying way up high
Lovely birds among the sky
Picture yourself floating there
Soaring, floating, everywhere

That is what this woman did
Airshow pilot, so legit
Bessie Coleman shocked the world
Female pilot, awesome girl!

If she did not have confidence
Her records would fail to exist
She flew and traveled far and wide
Talked of having so much pride

Made sure everybody knew
That Blacks were smart each time she flew
People came from everywhere
Honored her and showed they cared

She might have even tried to teach
Other girls to take her seat
But April 1926
Bessie took her final trip

Her plane, it crashed and then she died
Now she's an angel in the sky
Encouraged tons of other woman
Her impact, just the beginning

We were ready to move on
But something was now going wrong
Maya had to take a seat
Legs were hurting, and her feet

I got worried and was scared
But Mr. Leroy was prepared
He rolled her right into the hall
Had her breathe til' she was calm

I wasn't sure what I should do
So, I sat and waited too
Maya came right back to class
But ugh, the boys began to laugh

That's when Maya closed her eyes
Her tears were dropping, so were mine
I can't believe that kids can't see
How painful laughs and jokes can be

But then and there to my surprise
Maya simply dried her eyes
She pushed her chair right to the side
Continued talking, tons of pride

"The next woman we have for you
Her name's Mary Mcleod Bethune
If you thought Bessie was so great
Listen to what this lady made

The year was 1935
So much hate and much divide
The world was empty, incomplete
Until Bethune approached the scene

An activist who changed the game
Eased the Negro women pain
You know the *branch* we learned about
She made it right into their house

Worked for real life presidents
Her love for progress evident
An educator first at heart
Gave tons of women their first start

Among the things that she had done
A college, she created one!
She helped to move our world ahead
Mrs. Bethune was Heaven sent!"

We were done and kids had clapped
Maya was strong, nothing she lacked
Her confidence was through the roof
My mom would say she's bullet proof

I guess she taught us all today
No matter what people may say
You have to push through all the pain
Success is where you place your aim

Kelvin felt ashamed for sure
Maya's strength had reassured
That even disabilities
Can't stop someone from having dreams!

The day would end with one more group
Crunchy had to present, too
But Mr. Leroy called his name
And that's when he began to blame

"Hey, Charles, it is now your turn
You and your partner, what'd you learn?
Time to share your thoughts with us
Come up front, your turn, you must"

Crunchy heard and did not move
He was in such an awful mood
Lifted his heard and looked around
Began to squint his eyes and frowned

"Mr. Leroy…well see I--
Didn't get no sleep last night
Someone broke into our house
My project, I ain't figure out

I wanted to get it all done
Cleaned all night it wasn't fun
For real, though like I really tried
I tried to write the other night

Jamal and I got something done
Our lady's name was Jane Bolin
Around like 1939
She was a judge and saved some lives

But not like all the other ones
She was the first Black lady judge
So like, Bolin made history
Fought for all the kids like me

Made sure families were okay
She helped, the book said *advocate*
But like I said we aren't done
We need more time to finish up"

"Charles, your start sounds so great
Jamal, have anything to say?
I want you both to take the time
Two more days to get it right

Alright class that's it for now
Report cards, they will soon come out
Next week we begin review
Big State Tests are coming soon!"

Scene 14

The weekend came and April bloomed
Our big field trip would take place soon
This year we would make our way
To see all of the new displays

Museums are a special place
History that we can trace
We'll all get to go and learn
Before the trip there was concern

Mr. Leroy wrote a note
Sent it home for all our folks
The letter said that he regrets
That some kids can't come on the trip

He didn't list specific names
Behavior are what he had blamed
The letter mentioned things about
Forgiving kids but time ran out

April 3rd was now the date
The trip was planned and would take place
Crunchy, Kelvin and Jamal
Were all called out into the hall

At that point the class assumed
We all smirked and all said "oooooow"
Our teacher, he follows through
He does what he says that he'll do

"Morning, boys I hope you see
Maturity is what we need
Soon we will leave for our trip
Not sure you guys can come on it

There are rules we have in place
Rules you throw back in my face
We are running out of time
I don't want you three left behind

At times you don't listen to me
Fifth grade, not something to repeat
We have to finish off real strong
Learning must now carry on

If I let you come with us
You'll act like angels on the bus
And then, when we all walk around
Hands to yourselves, feet on the ground

I'm on your side but do you job
If not, for real…I'll call your moms!
Okay, but yes, I do believe
You boys are smart and can achieve!"

The boys agreed and came back in
Our teacher wants them all to win
People can hear from someone else
But have to want things for themselves

I have learned to work real hard
For my mom but most of all
I also want success for me
I have goals and *I* have dreams

It's only right for us to read
Always prepared, before we leave
Mr. Leroy asked us why
"Does this poem impact our lives?"

Langston Hughes created art
All of his poems come from the heart
Each time that he wrote a poem
You felt the pain all from his tone

Before we read it we all knew
This one, it would be powerful
Why else would we all read it now?
The message we'd find for ourselves

"Okay, class let's read alone
Once you finish, take some notes
If you have some challenges
Take your time, read it again"

"Mr. Leroy, man it's hard
Can you put notes up on the board?
Don't know what this man talkin' bout!
Can we just read the poem aloud?"

One of the kids just failed to try
He didn't even blink an eye
Before he even took a chance
He quit and had no confidence

"If you never even try
How will you ever win in life?
Don't give up please try again
If that don't work, I'll help you then"

I read the poem and, in my mind
I saw the words all come alive
Immediately understood
A letter written for manhood

Not a man but all of us
A world he tried to warn us of
Explained how hard things were for him
Could not ignore not one of them

Life had been no fun at all
You can't quit, you must carry on
Showed how strong we all can be
If you fight for what you believe

After we had time to write
Our teacher stood right by my side
Asked if I could read the poem
Of course I'll read, he should have known

Langston Hughes: Mother to son

"Well, son, I'll tell you:
Life for me ain't been no crystal stair.
It's had tacks in it,
And splinters,
And boards torn up,
And places with no carpet on the floor—
Bare.
But all the time
I'se been a-climbin' on,
And reachin' landin's,
And turnin' corners,
And sometimes goin' in the dark
Where there ain't been no light.
So boy, don't you turn back.
Don't you set down on the steps
'Cause you finds it's kinder hard.
Don't you fall now—
For I'se still goin', honey,
I'se still climbin',
And life for me ain't been no crystal stair"

At that point I knew for sure
I was right, but there was more
The speaker wanted us to know
That we can't quit, have far to go

Also, what I got from it
When life is hard, no time to sit
If we stop and sit to cry
Life don't stop, keeps moving by

So, I now know why we should
Sometimes life's misunderstood
Guess my mom must live by this
Climbs those stairs each chance she gets

Mr. Leroy added on
Explained just why he picked the poem
"When I was ten, I heard a rhyme
From a song that made me cry

Words had said he saw no change
Had to find some better ways
People that looked just like us
Live tough lives and need more love"

That's right when he turned it on
Hit the button, played the song
Closed his eyes and dropped his head
We all heard just what it said...

Changes by Tupac Shakur

"I see no changes…
Wake up in the morning and I ask myself
Is life worth living is what I ask myself?
I'm tired of bein' poor and even worse I'm black
My stomach hurts so I'm lookin' for a purse to snatch
Cops don't care about a negro
Pull the trigger kill a brotha he's a hero
Don't help support the kids and nobody cares

One less hungry mouth on the welfare
First take away hope, nobody healing brothers

Give 'em guns step back watch 'em kill each other
It's time to fight back that's what Huey said
Two shots in the dark now Huey's dead
I got love for my brother, but we can never go nowhere
Unless we share with each other
We gotta start makin' changes
Learn to see me as a brother instead of two distant
strangers
And that's how it's supposed to be
How can the Devil take a brother if he's close to me?
I'd love to go back to when we played as kids
But things changed, and that's the way it is

That's just the way it is
Things will never be the same
That's just the way it is
Aww yeah"

The song had been so powerful
Nothing else for us to do
Placed us all in different moods
Our lives, we wanted to improve

Time had come to take the trip
Long day left, well most of it
Walked in lines up to the front
That's when we got onto the bus

As the driver drove us there
In my head I still could hear
Words from Tupac's famous song
Reassured violence was wrong

"That's just the way it is...Things will never be the same..."

That is when the bus had parked
Time to get off and to start
Visiting this special place
We'll see history today!

The building was so beautiful
Gorgeous bricks and lovely stone
Soon as we got off the bus
Security then lined us up

Mr. Leroy scanned our pass
We walked in, they checked some bags
African American
Things in there were interesting

Several floors where do we start?
Marathon, get on your mark
We had things we had to find
List was long would take some time

Eight of us were in my group
Split the work best thing to do
Some of us would search for things
Stuff was so inspiring

By the time we seen enough
We were all ready for lunch
Can't use the cafeteria
Designated area

No food in and no food out
Was something that we talked about
We were not alone at lunch
Other schools were close to us

Just before I took a bite
I heard my name called from nearby
I looked around and tried to see
Who was it that called for me?

Standing there to my surprise
Were kids from a former time
My old school was on the trip
They had come same time we went!

Such a cool coincidence
But what I heard then made me sick
"Hey Alyah, is that you?
How are you, how do you do?

Your classmates they all look like you
We think that's why you left our school!
Not just that, but we all knew
That you needed more money too

I guess those are the reasons why
You'll never have a life like mine
Wish your life wasn't so tough
But either way we wish you luck"

I couldn't think, I was confused
What was it that she tried to prove?
I knew that kids at my old school
Were filthy rich, thought they were cool

But honestly my mom explained
Kids who bragged were actually lame
To think that money makes you strong
To feel that way is truly wrong

Our lives may not be the same
But my skin was not to blame
Being from my neighborhood
Gave me more than money could

I know people want to be rich
But who defines just what that is?
Buying stuff and having things
Won't help us change the pain we've seen

The girl she spoke, and she believed
That school is what helps you achieve
But what I learned throughout the year
Success can happen anywhere

I thought she spoke and finished up
Another joke, oh here it comes
She fixed her face at me again
She noticed something different

"Oh my goodness, that's so cute
Is that something Black girls do?
Wearing earrings even if
You don't know where the other is?

Why are you just wearing one?
It kind of looks silly and dumb
But again, maybe because
You can't afford the other one?"

I tried ignoring what she said
But her words stuck in my head
"It kind of looks silly and dumb
Can't afford the other one?"

At that point I don't know why
Closed my eyes tried not to cry
Not because of what she said
Because it's lost and can't find it

I lost the hoop, the power's gone
Without it, hard to carry on
The rule had mentioned what to do
Lose a hoop and dreams are through

But now was not the time to cry
I turned to her, opened my eyes
Told her that it just fell out
Didn't notice until now

Didn't need to open up
About my hoops and what they were
Her comment made me think to try
My hoop I still should try to find!

Most kids I know would be upset
And be sad from what she said
I truly saw she doesn't know
That struggle helps your strength to grow

There was a time that I believed
That being Black was hard to be
And now that I can see the truth
My skin is really bullet proof

Say whatever that you feel
My heart is strong and made of steel
To love and give helps make us rich
I only wish the girl knew this

And when all of my dreams come true
I'll give back like I plan to do
Unity and tons of love
Protection that comes from above

My neighborhood is home to me
No need to leave to feel complete
Community matters the most
Not private schools and fancy clothes

"Thank you for wishing me luck
You'll need it too, that you can trust
One thing that I will say to you
Rich is what you say and do

Money might feel good to have
But giving back is what will last
So, when you get back to school
Make respecting other cool"

The girl she turned away real slow
Her teacher called for them to go
She looked back and she said to me
"You're really smart, forgive me, please"

Scene 15

After lunch we all returned
Had a few more things to learn
Our chaperone, she led the way
Bottom floor to honor slaves

Elevator led us down
We were stories underground
It was sad and made me think
How did humans let this be?

Several hundred years ago
Africans thrown onto boats
They really did not know why
Forced to go or else they'd die

This happened for centuries
So many lives hard to believe
How could people sleep at night?
Knowing that this wasn't right!

White men were the ones in charge
Hate and fear was in their hearts
But then some chose to deny
Hate they learned from racist times

These men served to help the Blacks
Abolitionists, in fact!
There were men and ladies, too
Helped see free slaves make it through

Made our way from floor to floor
So much pain, hard to ignore
The poem we read before we left
Was now repeating in my head

Made me think of Langston Hughes
And how he knew which words to choose
These exhibits made me see
How powerful our poems can be

We made our way through most of it
One more section on our list
Up the stairs and to the top
Amazing clips we got to watch

We saw how TV started off
How Black actors had got involved
Sidney Poitier was cool
Harry Belafonte too!

Black people had done their best
Broke down walls and passed all tests
We saw those from then and now
Past and present, made me smile

Saw so many magic scenes
From slavery to Honorees
Next time when I think to quit
Our history, I'll think of it!

The time had come for us to leave
Things I saw made be agree
My mom had called me bullet proof
I now know why that phrase is true

During the month it rained a lot
Saw no signs of when it'd stop
We carried on and school was fine
Big state tests now on my mind

I thought of how I felt prepared
Before I had become aware
Until I broke the stupid rule
Without my hoop I'd fail at school

And now I feared falling behind
Negative thoughts all in my mind
I know it sounds so silly but
For some reason, the rules I trust

I spent the days searching around
But all the time did not amount
Or add up to make any sense
I lost the hoop and that was it

I gave up and I felt so bad
I lost the confidence I had
Why did it happen to me?
Where was it that I could not see?

Mr. Leroy gave review
Vocab words we had to do
He said that we would be prepared
But now the tests, I finally feared

One day at home I heard a sound
My mom was mad and really loud
Hung up the phone and suddenly
Came to my room to check on me

After almost ten whole years
She mentioned words I feared to hear
Said that someone made some plans
To come see us and take a chance

She hesitated to decide
If she'd say no or swallow pride
Told me that it was my choice
Hard to choose without her voice

"Your dad says that he wants to try
Wants to see you and come by
Told him that he better bring
More than just apologies

I made sure he knew that you
Do just fine, with just us two
So sometimes in life we learn
Maybe we give your dad a turn?"

The next few days were difficult
Felt like lumps were in my throat
Sometimes during class I cried
And my grades, some fell behind

Distracted by so many things
My hoop, my dad, my faded dreams
In my mind nothing made sense
How the good things came and went

Back when Ms. Brown chose to leave
Was unsure how the year would be
All I knew was time would tell
But recently my efforts fail

It seemed no matter what I did
None of it I seemed to fix
My mom was sad, life seemed to change
At that point I became afraid

One afternoon when I got home
A car out front I hadn't known
My mom and I both walked to see
A man who barely looked like me

My mom well she knew right away
For me I still starred in his face
My jar had dropped, and it was time
To see my dad, this man was mine

The three of us walked in the house
Surrounded by the darkest clouds
I couldn't move I couldn't talk
My mom said move, I couldn't walk

The man was now right in our home
Different skin, a different tone
The first thing I seen and thought
He did not look like me at all

His skin was white but kind of tan
That I did not understand
His hair was curly blonde and brown
Thought he'd look more like men in town

I thought back to when I was young
What I thought I knew was gone
Not sure If I remembered if
He was Black or looked like this

All I knew was that was why
My mom has darker skin than I
I don't mind because I know
Every race is beautiful

Before I even said a word
He began and had the nerve
I was raised to show respect
But would reject the words he said

"It's hard for me to face the facts
I've stayed away but now I'm back
I hope you know that you are loved
I'll try my best to earn your trust

Things you may not understand
I failed to even take a chance
Feared your mom would fail to see
It wasn't you, was always me

I know that you would both agree
Your mom is strong and so unique
But something made me change my mind
A feeling from way deep inside

You are the only child I have
So sorry haven't been your dad
I pray you let me in your life
I'll do my best I swear I'll try"

"I'm unsure what to do or say
It's always been just mom and me
I don't know why you left us here
But mommy raised me not to fear

So, if you think you're saving me
My mom raised me courageously
I beat the boys in all we do
I even get straight A's in school

If I were you, I'd go back home
And leave me and my mom alone
And one more thing just so you know
We could have said this on the phone"

I think I caught him by surprise
At that point tears had filled his eyes
Was what I said too much for him?
My honesty from deep within

My mom she had been standing near
His response is what she feared
What would he then say to me now?
Stared but words did not come out

His eyes were wet and fluttering
How hard he cried made me believe
That somewhere in his heart and mind
He'd die to have me in his life

And just before he spoke again
My mom she came, and she stepped in
Told us both to close our mouths
And how someday we'll work it out

That ended his first attempt
Left the house and off he went
Back to New York to live his life
I thought of him all day and night

My year began to fall apart
Felt like a dagger poked my heart
I started struggling more in class
Then one day Mr. Leroy asked

"Hey Alyah, can we talk?
I feel there may be something wrong
Do the boys still bother you?
Is there something I can do?"

At first, I failed to open up
But I had no one else to trust
I told my teacher all my thoughts
And if he ever felt this lost

"Mr. Leroy, I don't know
All my dreams I have let go
I can't ball and grades are bad
And I'm sad about my…"

Almost told him everything
I froze and kept some thoughts with me
Didn't know the reason why
That's when all I could do was cry

But Mr. Leroy was unique
Was brilliant and knew everything
Instead of asking why I cried
He talked about some lady's life

"Okay, Alyah tell me this
Do you know what NASA is?
Have you ever thought about
How rockets make it off the ground?

Take a problem that you have
Something that can make you sad
Imagine that there was a way
To solve the problem now, today!

Long ago no one believed
That space travel could be achieved
Scientists had given up
Smartest people were all stuck

But a woman, young and brave
Exceptional in many ways
Helped to integrate a school
Many things had made her cool

But this one thing that she knew
Hard for scientists to do
But it was not hard for her
Space travel, she'd make it work

Katherine Johnson was her name
She wasn't searching for the fame
She was a genius yes for sure
The reason why space is explored

I hope you see from hearing this
Impossible does not exist
When things seem so far out of reach
Continue finding missing links

Whatever that your problems are
Solutions, they lie in your heart
You will make it through them all
Stand back up each time you fall"

That afternoon when I got home
My mom spoke in a different tone
Asked me to describe my day
To mention what had taken place

Wasn't sure just what to think
I thought of my entire week
Thought of how my grade had dropped
And problems I wanted to solve

So, I took a real deep breath
Faced my mom and then I said
"I hate everything right now
School, the boys nothing works out

I lost my hoop, my dream is gone
The court is still where I belong
But you won't give me a chance
The *dad* thing I don't understand

I'm confused and sad and scared
I just wish that you could hear
How the kids at school go wild
From how I play when I'm allowed"

My mom sat there silently
Thought how to reply to me
I was sure to watch my tone
Respectfully had let her know

"Okay, now let's get this straight
School is now something you hate?
And the kids, still being rude
Even towards the end of school?

Why can't you ignore their jokes?
Focus on what matters most
And this thing about your dad
We will work through all of that!"

My mom was so quick to talk
Barely heard my words at all
I was sure to let her know
My feelings were out of control

"Well baby girl, you're all I've got
Tough problems we'll have to solve
Here's a message from today
Mr. Leroy called to say…

"Hello and good afternoon
Mr. Leroy…calling you
Quickly wanted to check in
To see, how Alyah's Been?

She has failed a quiz or two
Seen her crying in my room
Also has she mentioned why
She's been sad a couple times?

Either way I'm here to help
Don't feel like you're by yourself
If there's something I do
Let me know I'm here for you"

After my mom shared the call
I wasn't feeling bad at all
Mr. Leroy tried to help
Thought of us, not just himself

Scene 16

Later on my mom just sat
Recalled thoughts, reflected back
Was not quite sure what she felt
She took some time for herself

She asked God to help her solve
Problems that she did not cause
That's is why she sat alone
Spoke like God was on the phone

"God, what should I say and do?
Alyah has to make it through
It's early, her life just began
What decisions should I plan?"

My mom cried all through the night
She prayed for things to be alright
April's almost over now
With God, my mom will sure prevail

Next few days went by so fast
Reviewed all of the skills from class
The state tests were now on their way
No more time for us to waste

One more task we had to do
Would be tough but that we knew
Writing letters weren't hard
But the details brought up scars

"Alright class, this one is key
You'll all write letters to me
But they will address someone
From your past whose done you harm

Not like violence or a fight
Harm that has hurt from inside
What we write will show someone
We forgive something they've done

For example, here is mine
"Hey, hello…how's my dear wife?
I know that you didn't mean
Fussing, fighting or your screams

You were angry, that's alright
We should never have to fight
I love you and that's a fact
I forgive you, that is that!"

As our teacher finished up
Girls said "aww" and boys said "yuck!"
When we all stopped making noise
Things were clear, we got the point

Problem was I had no clue
Who to write my letter to?
If I wrote one to my mom
Not too sure what that would solve

Class was over still no name
Who harmed me, who could I blame?
Took some time and thought so hard
Had to really drop my guard

Later on, it came to me
Tossed and turned and could not sleep
Shot up quickly out of bed
My letter should be for my dad!

Two more days to hand it in
Spent the next day writing it
Failed to put words on the page
Was unsure just what to say

One more day and it was due
Tried to focus still no clue
Every time I wrote a word
Just felt more and more disturbed

Don't care if he apologized?
Never should have left my side
What on earth was I to do?
He doesn't love me I have proof

Spent ten years without him here
Had to mean he didn't care
But then why'd he come see us?
Maybe now it's safe to trust…

I sat down and tried again
Closed my eyes imagined him
Walking with me at a park
Holding hands, just for a start

Pictured him holding a ball
Shooting hoops and standing tall
Would place the ball right in my hand
Would tell me he's my biggest fan

This perfect day would never end
Spend all day just dribbling
As the sun would finally set
He'd finally tuck *Hoops* into bed

Thought of how nice that would be
Those thoughts led me to complete
My letter that I finished up
Showed me my dad could be loved

"Dear Dad,

I just turned eleven-years old and I am very smart. I have been to two schools so far in my life. Mom sent me to Elite Public Charter School when I was little and then I had the chance to go to the best schools in the country for a couple of years. But this year, I am back at my old school where I started because this place is free attend. I wonder if you were with me if I would have to go to this school? But I guess it's okay because I would not have had a chance to be in Mr. Leroy's class. Anyway, my teacher had us write a letter to someone and forgive them for harming us. At first, I didn't know who to write to but then I thought about it really hard and I thought of you. Mom never talks about you because I think she knows it might make me sad. But this is my letter to you and I am saying that it is okay now that you never came to see me or help me with stuff. Most kids at my school don't have their dads around either. I try my best at school and when I get older I am going to be in the WNBA. Not only that but I am going to help people and make the world a better place. I kind of think that a dad would want to be there if they had a kid like me. So even though I don't know why you don't help me I just want you to know that I forgive you and that I am sorry for being mean to you when you came to see me. Maybe you will read this and it will make you see how good I am and maybe you will want to come help me with stuff. My mom says that I am bullet proof so if you don't want to help me with stuff then I will keep being doing my best to help the world.

Love, Alyah Marie aka Hoops

The last assignment was complete
Finished my letter, wrote it neat
May was here, so much to do
A flyer posted in our room

During lunch the room was changed
Tonight was Daddy-Daughter Day
I was confused and sad inside
The other girls were full of pride

It seemed as if they'd all attend
The girls said that their dads loved them
How to feel I wasn't sure
My heart had broke and hit the floor

And just as I walked down the hall
The same tall man I'd seen before
My dad was here, he came again
I whipped my tears and ran to him

To see him was such a surprise
My mom is who gave him the ride
The two of them now standing there
My mom and dad, them both in tears

Mr. Leroy saw me run
About to yell but bit his tongue
He realized what was happening
He knew it'd make me feel complete

My letter had explained it all
Love, good grades, a chance to ball
Could not have been a better time
The Daddy-Daughter dance was mine!

That afternoon was something real
Alyah learned just how it feels
To be loved and to give it back
Not to a mom but to a dad

She bragged about all that she knew
The kids all seemed to like him too
He was so nice and so polite
He treated everyone just right

The next few weeks would go just smooth
Alyah fixed her grades in school
And when the state tests had begun
She smiled and aced all of them

My dad came back and forth a bunch
Tons of times we shared our lunch
We even went and hit the courts
I got my skills from him for sure!

He was so good at shooting threes
He also dunked with such an ease
I never thought I'd see the day
That me and my own dad would play

In the middle of the month
Dad took me out again for lunch
We sat down while we ate our food
Took out a letter, changed his mood

He went from glad to happier
Before had got what he deserved
But now this second time around
We shared our thoughts and worked it out

He took a breath and then he read
All of the words my letter said
At the end he whipped his eyes
Told me what his life was like

By the end it all made sense
Explained my mom was Heaven sent
But things he feared he had to fight
Was tough for him because he's White

Most of it was hard to hear
He loved my mom more every year
But back before he grew the strength
His family did not think the same

He told me some people don't see
The beauty that's in ***unity***
Mentioned just one reason why
His family told him not to try

My dad regrets the choice he made
He left and has himself to blame
"The wrong people can't help you choose
When you know right that's what you do"

After what I've learned from him
The pain I had left with the wind
My life it seemed to be complete
But one more thing was hurting me

May was great but not enough
Still missing one thing that I loved
Grades were fine, dad in my life
But without hoops, it wasn't right

I thought back to the tryout dates
AAU would soon take place
Tried to ask my mom again
Last time I begged her to no end

But I had nothing to lose
Blamed it on my missing hoop
If I hadn't lost that thing
Maybe I'd be on a team?

I don't think it works that way
More time passed, my dream felt fake
Maybe I was seeing things
Wishing and imagining

How do earrings just appear?
Gold can't just come from thin air
Either way this was my chance
Time to ask and take a stance

One morning I came downstairs
Had my argument prepared
But before I said a word
My mom had spoke and stole my turn

"Oh, hey girl good morning love
Have some fruit and juice because
Later on, this afternoon
There's something that you have to do"

"But mom please, listen to me"
"Girl don't talk, trust…you will see
And your dad is coming too
Go eat because he'll be here soon"

Just when I had thought to try
She talked more, attempt denied
But what was this chore of mine?
I wish that I could just decline!

My dad came just like she said
Came and sat down, face was red
Why were they both smiling?
Heard something hard to believe

Today was a special day
I was sure ready to play
Dad took out an orange box
My smiling could not be stopped

In the box were brand new kicks
Jordan sneakers, perfect fit
First pair that I'd ever have
Thanked my mom and hugged my dad

Tried them on and grabbed my ball
Faked a shot against the wall
But inside the orange box
A picture he must have forgot

Dad showed mom and then showed me
Pointed out just who he'd seen
"This guy is my brother Mike
He played ball, he was alright

But this guy he was the truth
Shot was fire, melted hoops
Game so hot made some rims sizzle
Was so quick and dude could dribble"

At that point my mom had cried
Couple tears then dried her eyes
Seconds later, she was fine
Then she quickly checked the time

"Okay, y'all…it's time to move
Alyah grab your shorts and shoes
We'll leave now to beat the rush
You'll love this, believe me…trust"

On the ride I had a thought
Of the picture that I saw
Uncle Mike and dude named *Sizzle*
Name stood out more than a little

As we drove it crossed my mind
Sizzle…Sizz it all aligned
That's when I just had to ask
Someone knew, my mom or dad

"So, I have something to ask
Were the guys friends from the past?
If so, who were they to you
Not Mike, but the other two?"

Silence met me once again
So far, no response from them?
Just when I had given up
My mom turned and cleared her throat

"Yes, of course that picture is
Of my bro, we called him Sizz
He's the one who lost his life
He played ball all day and night

What made it hard to believe
Why it was hard to agree
That you had a right to play
Overtime my thoughts have changed"

I was shocked in disbelief
Who'd she say he was to me?
Better yet what was his name?
Sizzle…Sizz, it was the same!

My eyes popped right out my head
Held my breath from what she said
Was it even possible?
Real life trip right through the snow?

Had to put those thoughts aside
Curiosity I'd hide
Later on, after this trip
I'll figure out who Sizzle is!

Shook my head and cleared my mind
My mom now stared in the eyes
Looked around couldn't believe
At the gym, was this for me?

"So today I'm proud to see
Show your skills to make the team
We are here for AAU
Get in there, do what you do!"

We pulled up, parked at the gym
Grabbed my bag and sprinted in
Read the signs and laced my sneaks
Girls in here I knew I'd beat

Coaches split the gym in two
Several groups to pass and shoot
Girls were on the smaller side
Boys need room had longer strides

During drills I played my best
My skills left my mom impressed
Every time I touched the ball
The kids and coaches were in awe

Sweat was rolling down my face
Feeling could not be replaced
Finally free, the cage unlocked
Flew like a bird amongst her flock

Unafraid to spread my wings
Life was great I loved the breeze
Highest heights is where I felt
So warm that my heart could melt

Not alone pursuing dreams
Loved that we all worked in teams
Built up tons of confidence
Time to play my very best

One cool thing about the sport
You get to help out on the court
If someone can't dribble then
I'll lead the way for us to win

And if I can't guard someone
Teammates help me, 2 on 1
Working together every time
Teamwork is a sacrifice

To be the best and earn the fame
You might endure a little pain
By digging deep then you can say
You gave your best during the game

Time moved on heard someone say
"That girl thinks she's better than me"
Dark skinned girls kept to themselves
White girls left me on the shelf

During breaks I was alone
And when girls took out their phones
None of them asked for my name
Wished they saw me as the same

But one group made fun of me
Other girls followed their lead
Black girls said I talked too smart
White girls wouldn't let me start

If I played and showed respect
Maybe then we'd all connect
How could I change how they act?
Played hard, showed I had their back

Whatever they thought of me
Would not let me feel defeat
My goal was to make the team
Maybe then the hate would flee

Sports have minds all of their own
Can erase hate and change your tone
By playing all on the same team
Shows racism can be beat!

Had a blast as time flew by
Mom and dad had watched with pride
Coaches all knew who I was
At tryouts I had caused a buzz

Had never been so confident
Was sure my effort was well spent
Coach said that the team would call
To place you on their team to ball

All night long sat by the phone
When it got late waited alone
I fell asleep, opened my eyes
At that point it was morning time

I checked the phone, and no one called
No message and it broke my heart
Maybe my mom had messed it up?
Maybe my dad ruined my luck?

No call left me in disbelief
It meant I did not make the team
All that I did and all I tried
Not on a team and wondered why

That night my mom just held me tight
Told me next season I can try
But what she did not understand
Was basketball's part of my plan

Those that get a chance to play
The same as warriors to me
Basketball's more than a sport
The way you shoot and crash the boards

Fighting for the chance to win
Every moment in suspense
The world watches your every move
Being the best is what you prove

But once games come to an end
People change from deep within
Seeing players sacrifice
Helps others improve their lives

Like others in history
Basketball makes us believe
Players are who play the game
But heroes are who some became

Unsure what the week would bring
Alyah thought the phone might ring
One day as she dressed for school
Saw a letter on the stool

Almost let it sit right there
But somehow knew she had to hear
Opened it and then she read
Thought it was for mom instead

At that point she took a chance
Mom might slap it out her hands
Ignored thoughts of punishment
She began, read all of it

"Dear Alyah,
So I hope by now you know
Your hoops the ones, made of pure gold
Were presents from me and here's why
Reminders so you'd always try

Those earrings, no power at all
The power's in your brain and heart
I gave them to you, so you'd learn
Be honest and you'll have your turn

You tried hard to trust the rules
You lost one, but still pursued
Never quit on things you loved
So proud of you from up above

And now you see that you are strong
Here's the hoop, now carry on!"
Love, your uncle Sean
aka Sizzle or Sizz for short

The letter left Alyah shocked
She almost jumped right out her socks
Reread the words and almost fell
Could not believe it was for real!

She realized just who Sizzle was
Her uncle Sean from up above
Her and mom then left the house
The note, she tucked it in her blouse

Reached for her bag, to her surprise
Her hoop was right there safe inside
Alyah had both earrings back
She wore them both and was so glad

Her and her mom jumped in the car
But they did not leave the yard
Took a breath and said a phrase
"What comes I'll be so brave"

Then her mom's phone rang aloud
Someone called and they both smiled
Both their eyes lit up like stars
Clueless sitting in the car

That's when they answered the call
Right on time, who would have thought?
"Good morning, is this time okay?
"Name's Coach Greg, I called to say

Last week, saw Alyah Play
Had to call, here's what I'll say
No guys can even come near
She had all the boys in fear

All the coaches do believe
Your daughter is who we need
I coach boys so this is new
She's the best, and that is true

She's amazing, so unique
Is she there with you to speak?
We need her and that's the truth
That girl, she can surely hoop!"

A Special Thank you...

On a cold October afternoon, my stomach was twisting and turning with anxiety. I was only ten years old, and yet, I had been exposed to more opportunities to assume adult-like responsibilities than most twenty-year-olds are given. I was often responsible for making sure my two siblings and I, at the time, made it to school before 7:45 a.m every morning. I was more often than not the person checking to make sure the three of us had clean clothes for the next day and that our homework was done the night before school. And more importantly, to mention, I was responsible for keeping us safe.

On that winter-like afternoon back in 1997, I was living the life of being one of the top youth football players in my town for the past two years. As a young athlete, football was one of the only things in my life that I seemed to have success with. Therefore, the opportunity of achieving my goal at one day becoming a professional football player was what I held onto the most. I was determined and had all of the intentions in the world on keeping that momentum for myself going.

Although I had the potential for being a young superstar in the making, one thing was determined to keep me from achieving my goals. Throughout my childhood, my mother didn't have a car. This often caused my siblings and I to miss out on several extracurricular opportunities. From our school to the playing fields, I could remember everything being very far away and out of walking distance.

Missing practices and making excuses for not being able to participate in activities several miles away from my home would have been understandable. But as life would go on, I came to find out that by not allowing obstacles to stop me from maximizing my chances to achieve great things, and by never giving up hope even when things aren't going my way, that at some point a window of opportunity will come by.

So on that cold, damp afternoon in October of 1997, as a ten-year-old football player and big brother, I walked for five miles to practice with my youth football team that day. And about one hundred feet from the parking lot, I was approached by a car. Driving was the father of a family whose son played on my team, and they asked me how long I had been walking. And what I remember telling them was that I didn't know for sure, but I knew that I didn't want to miss my opportunity to be the best football player in town this season. As chance has it, and commonly for many families around the country, I became the kid who the Weiss Family always picked up and brought home from practice.

From that day on, I saw the power in taking action. I chose to be accountable and to never use excuses for the lack of opportunities to improve my life. Instead, I realized that by showing effort and trying your hardest to get the job done, that it would always maximize my chances at a positive future for my own life.

By identifying open windows of opportunity, it is never too late to find a way out of no way. My mother was only two more practices away from pulling me off of that team because of her not knowing how she was going to provide safe and adequate transportation for her first son. But perhaps walking, as safe of a route as I knew, I somehow showed my dedication and passion to the world, which changed the trajectory of my life for the better. And in 2009, after completing four years of college, receiving two degrees and participating as a full-scholarship athlete, I thank those who stopped along the road who offered me a ride. Life...what a ride it will be.

ABOUT THE AUTHOR

Glen Leroy Mourning was born on March 26th, 1987, in Danbury, Connecticut. As the oldest of his mother Lillian's five children, Glen was blessed with the opportunity to lead by example where he would become the first of two generations to not only graduate from high school but to complete a master's degree.

In 2005 Glen earned a Full- Athletic Scholarship to attend the University of Connecticut, where he would make the All-Big

East Conference Academic Honor roll for two years in a row before graduating and attending Grad School at the University of Bridgeport.

In 2010 Glen finished his master's degree in Elementary Ed. and was named the student-teacher of the year at the University of Bridgeport. Since then, Glen worked alongside the nationally renowned Educational contributor Dr. Steve Perry, Star of the CNN Special "Black in America II" and the host of TV One's "Save our Sons."

As a 4th and 5th grade teacher at Capital Preparatory Magnet School in Hartford, Connecticut, Glen managed to brilliantly inspire the lives of hundreds of students in his tenure as an educator. At the same time, he was the assistant varsity football coach at Capital Prep, where the team posted an incredible record of 22-2, winning State playoff appearances before stepping down from his role as the defensive backs coach.

For the past year, Glen has worked in Washington D.C as a 4th grade teacher. Glen and his wife Nicole will continue working together in education in Washington, D.C., where they hope to continue writing and sharing literature for young people in America.

Glen's greatest accomplishments are not those that have occurred on the playing fields across America. Instead, he is most proud of his promise to his family that he has kept, which was to become the motivation for his students that come from similar circumstances.

More from the Author

Crunchy Life Book 1: Recess Detention

In book 1 of the Crunchy Life Series, students are challenged to think about what challenges they face daily that may distract them from being the best that they can be. Students often face problems that can easily overwhelm them, but what may also be hard for a kid to communicate to adults. Keep track of how Crunchy attempts to make smart choices in a confusing and challenging world. When times are tough, be sure to find positive people to surround yourself with.

Crunchy Life Book 2: Naughty or Nice

In book 2 of the Crunchy Life Series, students are challenged to think about times where they have had to serve a consequence after making a poor choice. Students often struggle with feeling as if they are bad kids. But in reality, sometimes kids make "bad" choices. Keep track of how Crunchy responds to his challenges. Always make good choices to avoid being naughty.

Crunchy Life Book 3: Tough Cookies

In book 3 of the Crunchy Life Series, students are challenged to have an open mind and hear from multiple perspectives. Students often struggle with learning new information, especially if it goes against what adults tell them. Keep track of how Crunchy grows as a thinker, as well as how he builds his confidence. Always be willing to learn new things!

Crunchy Life Book 4: One Piece at a Time

In book 4 of the Crunchy Life Series, students are challenged to differentiate between huge life problems and smaller problems that can be handled with coping skills. Students often struggle with thinking that no one understands how they feel. The truth is, adults want students to learn how to persevere. Keep track of how Crunchy pushes through tough situations. Always accept responsibility for your actions.

Crunchy Life Book 5: Every Point Counts

In book 5 of the Crunchy Life Series, students are challenged to be honest with themselves about whether or not they give 100 percent in the things that they set out to accomplish. Students often feel as though they are trying their best, especially on the things that they care about. However, with a little self-reflecting, students can find ways to dig deeper to improve their lives even more. Keep track of how Crunchy realizes that he has more in him on his way to success. Always give life your best shot.

Crunchy Life The Prequel: The Dream Chaser

In the prequel of the Crunchy Life Series, titled The Dream Chaser students are challenged to be honest with themselves about whether or not they give 100 percent in the things that they set out to accomplish. Students often feel as though they are trying their best, especially on the things that they care about. However, with a little self-reflecting, students can find ways to dig deeper to improve their lives even more. Keep track of how Crunchy realizes that he has more in him on his way to success. Always give life your best shot.

Care More Than Us: The Young People's Guide to Success and student work book.

"Care More Than Us" is a conversation style read for young readers and teenagers alike, who may have trouble identifying how great they or their students and children already are. By readjusting what it means to be successful, "Care More Than Us" takes the readers through the process of learning to believe in themselves and avoiding the crowd that may distract them from reaching their goals.

<u>Strategies to handle "crunchy" situations.</u>

When life seems challenging and things aren't going your way, remember that if you stay positive and calm that you will be alright.

1. **Ask yourself why you're angry (problem solve).** If you ask yourself why you're angry, and really think about your answer, you might figure out a problem you can solve or even uncover some of the sneaky feelings that feel like anger.

2. **Use "if-then" statements to consider the consequences.** If-then statements mean that you ask yourself what might happen if you do something. They are best used when you are deciding what to do about a situation or problem. If-then statements help you make better choices by helping you understand the consequences of your actions.

3. **Count up to or down from 10.** Sometimes, quietly counting to 10 is something some people do to stop themselves from doing something too quickly. Counting to 10 as soon as you notice you're having an angry reaction can give an angry person just enough think time to make sure their first idea is a good idea. If it's not a good idea, it can be just enough time to change it into a better one (reconsider).

4. **Listen to another person.** If you're angry about something or with someone else, talking to someone and listening to their perspective— even the person you're angry with—may help you understand exactly what caused the problem so you can fix it or figure out what you can do in the future to prevent the situation.

5. **Focus on your breathing.** Focusing on breathing can help during angry moments in several ways. First, it takes your attention away from the anger for a moment, just like when you count to 10. Second, breathing in a certain way, slowly and deeply (so deeply that your belly moves, too), and in through your nose and out through your mouth, can often help people who are angry to begin to calm down.

6. **Take a walk or step away.** Change the environment by taking a walk or stepping away if you can. Just like counting to 10, and thinking about your breathing, walking away from a situation that is making you angry can sometimes help prevent you from reacting to a situation too quickly, or it can give you some time to breathe and think about good choices you can make.

7. **Give yourself some good advice (self-talk).** Self-talk means that you say to yourself the things that a good friend would say to calm you down, such as, "Calm down," "Maybe it's not that bad," or "Let it go." It is best used when

you first notice that you are angry (emotional reaction stage). Its purpose is to help calm you down. Use self-talk if you notice yourself using any thinking errors (use logic).

8. **Look for the humor—without making fun of someone.** Sometimes we get angry for silly reasons that are hard to explain. Maybe you don't even really want to be angry. Sometimes, if there is no danger, you can count to 10 and imagine what it must look like if this whole angry situation was something you were watching in a TV comedy. Sometimes, when you really think about it, some of the things that make us angry can seem really silly. Remember, though, that if you are involved in an angry situation with someone else, they may not think it's funny at the same time you do. It usually works best if you can laugh at yourself.

Source: https://blog.brookespublishing.com/8-anger-management-tips-for-your-students/

Submit your Crunchy Conversation Testimonials to mourningknows@gmail.com and share with author Glen Mourning how you faced a challenging situation and how you were able to persevere.

For more information, visit www.glenmourning.com.

Made in the USA
Monee, IL
19 February 2021